From *The Grey Mist Murders*

Lady Marsh joined us at that point and ordered a cock-tail for herself. She immediately took the floor with her piercing voice, as she always did.

"Do you know," she said, "every morning when I come out of my cabin I find three matches lying on the floor, just over the sill—and always in the same position. I pick them up and throw them out the port, and then there they are the next morning again. They look like the same matches every time too. I'm beginning to get nervous about it."

Books by Constance & Gwenyth Little

The Grey Mist Murders (1938)
The Black Headed Pins (1938)
The Black Gloves (1939)
Black Corridors (1940)
The Black Paw (1941)
The Black Shrouds (1941)
The Black Thumb (1942)
The Black Rustle (1943)
The Black Honeymoon (1944)
Great Black Kanba (1944)
The Black Eye (1945)
The Black Stocking (1946)
The Black Goatee (1947)
The Black Coat (1948)
The Black Piano (1948)
The Black Smith (1950)
The Black House (1950)
The Blackout (1951)
The Black Dream (1952)
The Black Curl (1953)
The Black Iris (1953)

The Grey Mist Murders

By Constance & Gwenyth Little

From the collection of
Janette E. Horst
1921 - 2000

The Rue Morgue Press
Boulder, Colorado

Constance & Gwenyth Little

Although all but one of their books had "black" in the title, the 21 mysteries of Constance (1899-1980) and Gwenyth (1903-1985) Little were anything but somber affairs. The two Australian-born sisters from East Orange, New Jersey, were far more interested in coaxing chuckles than in inducing chills from their readers.

Indeed, after their first book, *The Grey Mist Murders*, appeared in 1938, Constance rebuked an interviewer for suggesting that their murders weren't realistic by saying, "Our murderers strangle. We have no sliced-up corpses in our books." However, as the books mounted, the Littles did go in for all sorts of gruesome murder methods—"horrible," was the way their own mother described them—which included the occasional sliced-up corpse.

But the murders were always off stage and tempered by comic scenes in which bodies and other objects, including swimming pools, were constantly disappearing and reappearing. The action took place in large old mansions, boarding houses, hospitals, hotels, or on trains or ocean liners, anywhere the Littles could gather together a large cast of eccentric characters, many of whom seemed to have escaped from a Kaufman play or a Capra movie. The typical Little heroine—each book was a stand-alone—often fell under suspicion herself and turned detective to keep the police from slapping the cuffs on. Whether she was a working woman or a spoiled little rich brat, she always spoke her mind, kept her sense of humor, and got her man, both murderer and husband. But if marriage was in the offing, it was always on her terms and the vows were taken with more than a touch of cynicism. Love was grand, but it was even grander if the husband could either pitch in with the cooking and cleaning or was wealthy enough to hire household help.

After writing a mainstream novel that put their own mother to sleep, the Littles turned to mystery fiction. Their first effort in this new direction was the present volume, *The Grey Mist Murders*, a shipboard mystery which drew heavily on their own experiences traveling around the world. First published in 1938, it has never been reprinted and is one of the

scarcest books in the genre. More than their later books it owes a debt
to Mary Roberts Rinehart and the Had I But Known school of mystery
writing, in which the heroine is frightened out of her wits for much of
the book and needs the steadying presence of a stalwart male to keep
her from going to pieces. But if the Littles had yet to find their true
voice in this first novel, there are already bits here and there that fore-
shadow the madcap antics that were to become their trademark: the
brittle dialog, the incessant drinking, smoking, and bridge-playing, the
unabashedly mercenary streak in the heroine, the elaborate planting of
clues and suspects, and the continued misunderstandings that keep stall-
ing the romantic subplot. Above all, it introduces a sophisticated and
spirited young heroine who has to solve a murder because she finds
herself the chief suspect.

The Littles wrote all their books in bed—"Chairs give one backaches,"
Gwenyth complained—with Constance providing detailed plot outlines
while Gwenyth did the final drafts. Over the years that pattern changed
somewhat but Constance always insisted that Gwen "not mess up my
clues." Those clues were everywhere and the Littles made sure there
were no loose ends. Seemingly irrelevant events were revealed to be of
major significance in the final summation.

The Littles published their two final novels, *The Black Curl* and *The
Black Iris*, in 1953, and if they missed writing after that, they were at least
able to devote more time to their real passion—traveling. The two made
at least three trips around the world at a time when that would have
been a major expedition. For more information on the Littles and their
books, see the introductions by Tom & Enid Schantz to The Rue Morgue
Press editions of *The Black Gloves* and *The Black Honeymoon*.

CHAPTER ONE

I HAD BEEN HOPING all night that it wouldn't rain when the boat got in at Tahiti—and it didn't. I'd collected the best specimen of man on board to go ashore with, and I wanted to wear the sort of clothes that simply cannot be exposed to rain. And I was very anxious to expose them to Peter Condit.

I got up rather early, when I discovered that the sun was shining, and dressed carefully. It had rained at New Zealand and part of the time at Rarotonga, and I'd had to dress accordingly, but now I felt that I could do myself justice and really show Peter how the modern, smart young woman should be turned out.

I knew the effect was good when I'd finished. After all, I'm young and slim and good looking—and I know how to dress. My guardian, Uncle Henry, says I'm vain and conceited because I admit it, but what is the use of clasping your hands and lowering your eyes and pretending you don't know it?

Uncle Henry and Aunt Edna have taken care of me since my parents died when I was a little girl. My father left me an income and a certain sum that was to be used for a trip around the world when I was twenty-five. Uncle Henry thinks I spend the income extravagantly and has spent the twenty years since my father's death in shaking his head over the trip around the world. It seems my father always insisted that travel was broadening and the best sort of education, but Aunt Edna says I was as broad—mentally—at fifteen as anybody should allow themselves to get.

Anyway, when the time came for my trip Uncle Henry gave his head a last shake and went into town and made all my reservations. He insisted on getting deluxe suites everywhere—I suppose with some idea of surrounding me with an aura of respectability, since I would not be chaperoned.

It was all right, too, except that it left me a bit short of spending money.

I was wondering, as I dressed that morning, whether Peter thought I was rich, because I was the only passenger with a deluxe cabin. I remember thinking, "What a sell for Peter, if that's the reason he honored me with his invitation to see Tahiti."

We were pretty close in when I went out on deck, and I hung over the rail and simply gaped. It was I the most beautiful sight I'd ever seen, I think. The water was turquoise, and the island dark green, with mist floating among the higher points.

Miss Merton was the only other passenger in sight. She never allowed herself to miss any of the sights, and she was trying to pick out Papeete through a pair of binoculars. She wore the white linen suit—that she must have laundered since Rarotonga—and it made her hips look as broad as ever. She had high-heeled white oxfords and a red beret pushed rather forward to make room for her big bun of dark hair. She was smoking a cigarette and had her mouth painted the same color as her beret, but it was no use. She still looked like what she was—a schoolteacher on a holiday. She was all ready to go ashore, of course, long before we would be able to—even to the camera hung over her shoulder.

I looked around for Mrs. Jennings and Mr. Imhoff and spotted them farther along the deck. I knew they'd be there because they were always ready for everything hours before it happened.

Mr. Imhoff was an elderly bachelor—a retired schoolmaster, I think. He always wore his rubbers and carried an umbrella, and he must have had a separate suitcase for all the pills and medicines that he hauled around with him.

Mrs. Jennings was a stuffy creature who was always quoting her absent husband and always referred to him as "the captain." We never found out what kind of a captain he was, and I guess none of us cared much. She never sat down without producing some knitting or a bit of fancy work for her son's children or her daughter's hope chest. Rumor had it that her daughter was already thirty-six but still hoping.

I said hullo to Celia Merton, and she smiled at me and said, "Isn't it delightful?"

I agreed and then could not think of anything else to say. But that was the trouble with Miss Merton—you never knew what to say to her.

We looked at the scenery for a while, and then the bugle blew for breakfast. Mrs. Jennings and Mr. Imhoff disappeared like magic—they were always the first down to meals—but Miss Merton kept her eyes determinedly on the island and looked as though she were counting up to a hundred. I expect she was hungry enough, but somebody must have told her it wasn't smart to go to the dining saloon as soon as the bugle blew.

After she had gone I began to feel pretty hungry myself, so I counted up to a hundred and then went down.

There were only twelve first-class passengers, and for a while, after I got down, there were only the four of us in the dining saloon. Then Chester Gordon came in. Chet wasn't terribly attractive, but he was a nice boy. He was an Australian, with plenty of Australian accent, and his father was in the grocery business. Papa was sending Chet to California to learn American methods.

He and Sally Grable and I sat at the doctor's table, and he was all agog over Sally's tanned face and pale gold hair and blue eyes. But I must say that the doctor seemed to prefer auburn curls and green eyes. My eyes are green, and if several people have compared them to cats' eyes I know why, and they needn't think I don't.

I said good morning to Chet and added unnecessarily, "Planning to go ashore?"

I wanted to know who he was going with. Or perhaps it's "whom." Uncle Henry could tell you.

Chet beamed and said happily, "I'm going with Sally. We're going to do the whole island—everything."

So that was how it was. Sally had taken Chet when she couldn't get Peter. I suddenly felt very cheerful. I said, "You'd better go and wake her up. Sally usually sleeps till noon."

He said he would and began to mess around with a couple of fried eggs. I leaned back in my chair and watched the Marsh family parade solemnly to the captain's table.

They were four in number—Sir Alfred Marsh, Lady Marsh, Miss Lucy Marsh and Miss Phyllis Marsh—and they hailed from New Zealand. They were going to New York, London and Paris, to give the girls some sort of finishing—and they needed plenty, poor things. They were terribly thin, had long faces and long, nondescript hair which, Sir Alfred maintained, was going to stay on their heads.

He said that a woman's crowning glory was her hair, and he used to get quite hot about it if anyone kindly suggested that the girls might try a long bob or something. He was a stuffy old fool, and Lady Marsh was an organizer. She organized the girls' clothes, which were the best things about them, but at that, they were quite hopeless. They couldn't even hold a social conversation, and yet the older one, Lucy, was pitifully boy crazy.

We all felt rather sorry for the captain, because they were all he had to talk to whenever he came down to a meal. But he was absent from the dining saloon quite often that trip, and nobody blamed him.

None of the officers appeared at breakfast that morning, and I knew we had our full quota of passengers, because the Widow Bayliss—who preferred to be known as Kay—and Peter never by any chance got up for breakfast.

I felt suddenly that the dining saloon had become a dull place for dull people. Celia Merton and Mr. Imhoff, who sat at the purser's table, were eating in absolute silence, and Mrs. Jennings, who sat with the chief officer, Kay and Peter, had a book on Tahiti propped up in front of her.

Lady Marsh was talking in a steady monotone and putting away more breakfast than the rest of her family combined.

I left them to it and went up on deck and sat on a deck chair and promptly fell asleep. I don't know how long I slept but when I woke we were almost in, and I found my particular gang all together and hanging over the rail. Dr. Barton was there, in a spotless white uniform; Peter, splendidly arrayed as usual and almost handsome into the bargain; Kay, in a bizarre sports costume; and Sally. Chet came up a few minutes later.

Sally looked wickedly attractive. She was only nineteen, and her parents, divorced years ago, had something to do with the moving pictures in California. She had been allowed to take the trip to Sydney and back entirely alone, and she'd had a wild time from start to finish. Poor Sally. She was so pretty and so gay.

When we were nearly ready to go ashore Mr. Imhoff suddenly became one of us, and I realized that Kay, feeling acutely the need of an escort and missing the doctor, who was not available for shore trips, had annexed the old fool. I had to stare hard at the deck for a moment to keep from laughing out loud.

We all went down the gangplank, followed by a few parting words of advice from Dr. Barton. I knew that Sally and Kay would stick to Peter and me like glue to avoid being left with their own dull escorts, but I knew, too, that Peter would shake them just as soon as he was ready—and I thought it would be pretty soon at that. He was a past master at the art of politely shaking people, and he had once told me that he would not dream of doing his sight-seeing in any sort of a crowd; it had to be only in the company of a charming woman or not at all.

As we stepped ashore I felt that everything was wonderful—the day, my mood, the whole setup.

And within twenty-four hours I was plunged into a black nightmare of horror.

CHAPTER TWO

PETER AND I RETURNED to the ship at about eleven that night, after having been to all the right places. Peter always went to the right places, and of course I was supposed to be properly impressed. But somehow, by the time we got back I was damned tired of it. There were so few right places in Papeete that we had to spend a long time in each one, and just drinking and trying to keep the conversation scintillating gets pretty boring—at least to me. I had wanted to take a drive out to Captain Cook's monument or the Grotto, but Peter came over superior and declared he detested sight-seeing in any shape or form, so that was that.

It is supposed to be an asset to be the last one back to the boat after a port visit—probably because it proves you have had a gay time or something, and if you had a gay time that in turn proves that you are attractive and can attract people who are capable of giving you a gay time. I don't know whether that is clear or not, but anyway, you can see what I mean.

Needless to say, Peter and I were the last on board, and as we came up the gangplank he made what passed for a witty remark, and I tinkled out a gay laugh, just to show how the day had gone.

Mr. Imhoff, Celia Merton and Mrs. Jennings were waiting anxiously near the gangplank for us. They always did that, because they had a horror of missing the boat. They themselves were always back hours before sailing time, and then they stood about and counted off the others as they returned. They usually got excited toward the end and seemed half to hope and half to fear that the last ones would be left behind.

As Peter and I stepped onto the deck the three of them seemed to relax. They murmured something about a close shave and then disappeared—probably to their cabins to lie down and rest after the strain.

Peter and I were getting pretty fed up with each other by this time, but we felt we had to keep up appearances until the end, so we went along to the bar for a last drink. We didn't want it—we'd had plenty—but it seemed a fitting finish.

As we stepped in at the door I was hard put to it not to gasp and stagger. At one of the tables was seated a man who would have taken anybody's eye, and I freely admit that he took mine completely. It's awfully hard to describe Robert Arnold without making him sound like a tailor's dummy or a movie hero, so I'll merely say that he was the most attractive man I'd ever seen.

Kay and Sally, of course, were draped on each side of him, and I noticed that Chet and Lucy Marsh were somehow on the edge of the group. Chet was sitting quietly and staring down at the drink in his hand, but Lucy was straining forward eagerly, trying to hear what was said and occasionally putting in an ineffectual word of her own.

I collected myself and glanced at Peter, only to find that he was as tranced as I had been. "Jealous," I thought. He must have known that this man could easily take his place as Most Desirable Male Passenger.

He began to move forward as though drawn by a magnet, and I moved with him. I was convinced that Kay and Sally had noticed us as soon as we appeared, but they completely ignored us and continued to chat brightly and laugh loudly.

I glanced at Lucy, and she said, "Hullo," rather stiffly, and at that point the stranger looked up at us inquiringly. Anyone would have supposed that Kay and Sally had never seen us before in their lives, and I was beginning to feel a bit silly when Lucy suddenly rose to the occasion, "Miss Bray, may I present Mr. Arnold? And Mr. Condit?"

Mr. Arnold arose, and Kay and Sally said unenthusiastically, "Hello, Carla. Peter."

Mr. Arnold said, "Won't you sit down, Miss Bray?', and I slid into his chair, knowing full well that those two women were hating me violently.

And that wasn't the worst of it, for no sooner had I settled comfortably than the fascinating Arnold declared he had had a tiring day and thought he would turn in—and away he went.

We sat on for a while, just for the looks of the thing, and made inane remarks about the weather. Chet sat down by Sally and talked to her for a while in a low voice, but she was obviously uninterested and even a little impatient. She presently stood up, yawned and declared that she was going to bed. Kay and I said it was a good idea, and the men drifted after us. We left Lucy sitting at the table, thin and drooping and a little disconsolate.

I walked down the first flight of stairs with Sally, who went on down another two flights, while I wended my way to my deluxe cabin. To my surprise I noticed that another of the deluxe cabins was occupied. The door was slightly open, and a light shone through the crack. I was curious about it, and I slowed down and tried to get a glimpse of the room, and at that very moment the door opened wide, and the Arnold man stood confronting me. He slightly raised his eyebrows and said, "Ah—Miss Bray."

I knew he was laughing at me and I felt confused and embarrassed. "I—I'm so used to having this section all to myself," I stammered foolishly. "I was just wondering . . . I mean, surprised . . ." I knew I was blushing, and I don't know when I've felt such a perfect idiot.

He said gravely, "I hope I'm not intruding too much."

"Oh no, I—I'm glad. I mean, it isn't so lonesome." I said good night and hurried off, but I could feel his eyes following me all the way to my door, and it was three doors from his. Just try to walk along a corridor with dignity when you're watched by someone who must think you are an utter fool!

I undressed and went to bed, but I did not feel sleepy, so I propped myself up with pillows and got a book and a box of candy. The book was interesting, and I did not listen consciously to any of the usual ships' sounds as we got under way again. I was merely vaguely aware of the throbbing of the engines and of the fact that we had started.

It was some time after that that I thought I heard Sally giggle. She had a high piercing laugh that you could not very well mistake, but I had read on for a full paragraph before I realized that I had heard it. I stopped reading for a moment then and thought it over. I knew that Sally's cabin was two decks below, and no one had a room anywhere near mine, so what could she be doing around these parts? It was funny.

Then I remembered the handsome Arnold and decided with a contemptuous sniff that she was visiting him. I knew that she was pretty wild and unconventional and probably would not think twice about a thing like that. I considered it for a while and then tried to dismiss it from my mind and hoped that I was properly indifferent about it. I went back to my book with a vague feeling that even Mr. Arnold's cabin was too far away for Sally's giggle to reach me.

I turned out the light a few minutes later. I noticed that the boat was rolling a bit, and I remember hoping that we were not in for a storm. As I dozed off I was conscious of a regular, heaving thud against what sounded like the door in my bathroom, which led into the next cabin. I listened to it drowsily for a while, but I was too comfortable to get up and investigate, and I presently drifted off to sleep.

CHAPTER THREE

I HAD A NIGHTMARE that night and woke shaking and sweating with fright. I lay still for a while looking around the cabin and trying to assure myself that all the familiar things were there and that everything was all right. I was beginning to relax when my eyes drifted to the little chair that ordinarily stood in front of the dressing table—and my heart seemed to stop for a minute, and then it began to beat furiously.

The chair had been moved. There was no doubt about it, because I had washed my stockings and hung them over its back before going to bed, and it had certainly stood in front of the dressing table then. Now it was beside the bathroom door.

I knew at once that the rocking of the boat was not sufficient to have done it. I felt an impulse to scream but stifled it somehow. I fumbled for the light with a shaking hand, and as it clicked on I heard that peculiar muffled thud again. I sprang out of bed and made a hasty search of the room. I was shaking all over, and my hands and forehead were wet.

The thud came again as I was searching the bathroom, and I tried the farther door, but it was locked. While I still had my hand on the knob it thudded again, and the bits and pieces of composure I'd managed to pull about me melted away like mist. I fled back into the cabin and stood shivering in the middle of the floor.

As soon as I was able to walk without my knees banging together I searched the room again and then feverishly locked the door and closed and locked the port which gave onto the deck.

I went back to bed and lay curled up, tense and quite unable to sleep. The room began to get terribly hot and stuffy, and the muffled thud came at regular intervals, until, with slowly growing horror, I began to feel that I was locked in with it.

That sent me out of bed in a panic again, and I unlocked the door and threw open the port.

The air was better almost immediately, and for some long time after that I lay listening for stealthy steps in the corridor and nervously watching the window for the appearance of some dreadful face or apparition.

But nothing happened, and after what seemed ages it began to get light. I felt a bit better as the black turned to grey, and I could see that there was nothing crouching in the corners of the room. I made a determined effort to go to sleep, but I could not free my mind from that regular thud on the bathroom door. I tried to tell myself that one of the stewards had left something hanging there, and I tried to feel annoyed with him for having done it. I would tell someone about it before I went down to breakfast, and I'd make quite a fuss about it too.

But I could not sleep, and it suddenly occurred to me that I might as well make my fuss now. My steward would be glum at being rung for at six o'clock, but after all, they shouldn't leave things hanging on doors where they could disturb deluxe passengers! I pressed the bell long and urgently.

There was a short wait, and then I heard footsteps, accompanied by a subdued grumbling. However, the knock was quiet and discreet, and when I called, "Come in," my steward stepped in the door and looked at me with polite inquiry.

"There's something in the next cabin, bumping against the bathroom door," I said fretfully. "It's been there all night, and I can't sleep. I wish you'd take it away."

He said, "Yes, miss," and backed out silently, but I could see that he thought I was making a silly fuss about nothing at an outrageous hour of the morning. I felt both guilty and indignantly self-righteous.

I heard him walk to the next door and rattle the handle, and the next instant he let out a hoarse cry.

I felt almost as though I had been expecting it. I sprang out of bed and ran along the corridor, struggling wildly to get my arms into my dressing robe. The steward was standing just inside the door of the next cabin, his mouth hanging slack and his eyes bulging. I stepped in behind him and looked over his shoulder.

I can't remember how I felt as I looked at it, but the sight is quite clear in my mind. Even today I dream about it still, sometimes, and wake up shaking and crying.

A human figure was hanging from an overhead pipe by a cord that seemed to be wound around and buried into its neck. It swung lazily with the roll of the boat and bumped the door to the bathroom at intervals. It wore an exquisite satin and lace nightgown, and a quilted satin dressing robe hung open from the shoulders. A pair of frothy bedroom slippers lay on the floor below, as though they had been kicked off. The face was quite dark and the eyes prominent and ghastly. It was only by the blond curls that I recognized Sally.

I guess I had hysterics. I don't remember much about it except that someone was screaming horribly, and I finally realized that it was myself. Then there were a lot of people around, and I seem to remember Mr. Arnold, but nothing is clear until some time later, when I found myself lying in my berth with a stewardess sitting grimly beside me.

I took a deep breath, sat up and asked shakily, "What happened?"

"You had better lie down and try to be calm."

"I'm perfectly all right," I said shortly. "I'm not usually hysterical. But that—that thing—I was here with it all night—and didn't know."

"Can't see that that makes any difference," she said coldly.

"It doesn't of course. But—oh, poor Sally!"

"Is that who it was?" she asked, her pale eyes lighting up with interest.

"Didn't you know?"

"I don't know anything about it," she said resentfully. "I had to take care of you from the start."

"Well, you're all through now," I told her crossly. "I'm all right, and I want to get dressed. You can go on out and snoop and come back and tell me what happened."

She trotted out eagerly, and I began to dress. I felt as though I'd been put through a wringer, and my head ached dully. It took me a long time, and I had just finished when the stewardess returned.

She had an air of subdued excitement about her, and she said smugly, "You're wanted in the captain's room, miss. They say Miss Grable couldn't have done it herself. She was murdered."

CHAPTER FOUR

A STEWARD LED THE WAY to the captain's quarters, and I followed him with a mounting sense of excitement. Sally murdered! And I'd heard her giggle! That giggle must have been just before it happened. But I hadn't heard her cry out or anything. I shivered and drew a little closer to the steward in front of me.

I remembered suddenly the chair in my cabin that had been moved during the night, and I gasped. The murderer must have been in my room!

The steward turned his head and asked, "Is anything wrong, miss?"

I shook my head, but I was walking so close to him by that time that I was nearly stepping on his heels.

The captain and the purser were talking together in low tones when I entered the captain's stateroom. The cord that had been around poor Sally's neck was lying on a table in front of them. It was a thick silk cord, and I realized that it must have come from her dressing robe.

The captain was a genial soul, well liked by everybody, but the purser was a gloomy, saturnine individual with a long face and an aggrieved manner. He seemed now, in some subtle manner, to be more pleased and contented with things than I had yet seen him. Nevertheless, his expression was as gloomy as ever. He asked me sadly to be seated.

The captain said, "Miss Bray?"

"Carla Bray," I replied, determined to have no misunderstandings.

"Yes. Well, a very serious thing has occurred."

I said hastily, "Yes, I know." Why on earth did he think I'd had hysterics if I didn't know that Sally had been murdered?

But he insisted on making his little announcement. "We are forced to the conclusion that Miss Grable was murdered. The only thing she could have been standing on when the cord was put around her neck is the chair. And that chair was placed over on the other side of the room. She could not have kicked it over there—the distance was too great— and in any case it would have been knocked over. So therefore—"

"She was murdered," I supplied brightly.

The purser frowned at me, and I felt like a fool.

"According to the testimony of the steward who found her," the captain continued, "the cabin wasn't disturbed in any way before the arrival of Mr. Ogilvie and myself . . . . And now we would like your story, if you please."

I told them all I knew, as carefully as I could. They seemed worried when I came to the part about the chair having been moved, and questioned me closely regarding it. They even called my steward and asked him if he had been in to close my port during the night, but he said he had not. They sent for Mr. Arnold then, and while we waited for him I found myself touching up my hair and smoothing down my dress.

He came in presently, looking freshly brushed and turned out and wearing a smart lounge suit. He said good morning to us and smiled at me in a peculiar way—it made me feel as though he and I had some guilty secret between us. I felt my face grow hot and turned away in time to see the expression of dark suspicion on the purser's face.

Mr. Arnold offered us all cigarettes and then lighted one for himself and sat down on the captain's bed. I took one, but the captain and the purser refused—Mr. Ogilvie, I think, because he felt that the situation was too grave for such informality, and Captain Lang, I am sure, because he did not want Mr. Arnold to smoke on his bed. His quarters were as neat as a pin, and I had heard that he was as fussy as an old lady about his housekeeping.

Mr. Ogilvie fastened a dark stare upon Mr. Arnold. "Miss Bray tells us that she heard Miss Grable laughing in your cabin last night."

"I didn't say any such thing," I cried hotly, but the purser waved me to silence.

Mr. Arnold glanced at me, and once again I was uneasy without knowing why. There was something in the expression of those inscrutable grey eyes—what was it?

He slightly raised his eyebrows at the purser and said, "If she did pay me a visit I was unaware of it."

"You deny, then, that she was in your cabin last night?"

"Hardly that," he said indifferently. "But if she was there I slept right through her visit."

"Did you hear anyone moving about at any time during the night?"

There was the faintest suggestion of a pause before he said with finality, "Nobody. The last thing I heard before I turned in was the airy click of Miss Bray's heels as she pushed on to her lair."

Captain Lang forgot himself and smiled faintly, but Mr. Ogilvie was beginning to feel like a district attorney or something, with his teeth in a bone, and he looked more forbidding than ever.

"How do you know they were Miss Bray's footsteps?" he asked cleverly.

Mr. Arnold had just dropped some ash onto the carpet, and he rubbed it in with his foot, while the captain eyed him balefully, before he said casually, "I opened the door and looked."

The purser seemed a bit crestfallen for a moment, but presently he brightened up, and he put all the district attorney he had into his next question.

"And do you always look out to see who it is when somebody passes your door?"

"Quite often," said Mr. Arnold sadly. "My mother has spent a great deal of her life sitting at a window behind a lace curtain, and I seem to be somewhat the same. Whether it is a matter of heredity or environment I could not say, but—"

The purser broke in on him coldly. "Then you claim that you heard nothing suspicious all night— even though a gruesome murder was committed very close to you?"

"Right," said Mr. Arnold. "I slept like the well-known log."

Mr. Ogilvie regarded us for a moment in suspicious silence, and then he asked Captain Lang if there were any more questions.

The captain, looking decidedly unhappy, said no, and Mr. Arnold and I went out together. We walked down the deck, and after a while he said, "Have you had breakfast?"

I was almost in tears, although I didn't exactly know why, so I merely shook my head.

He took me by the arm and steered me down to the dining saloon, and when we got there he sat down at my table. The chief steward came hurrying over and said that he had a place at the captain's table for Mr. Arnold.

Mr. Arnold smiled at him amiably and said that he really preferred it where he was, because there was a better view of the sea.

The chief steward was visibly upset and gave voice to a polite protest—I think he hated to have his neat little arrangements disregarded—but Mr. Arnold was firm.

"The captain will like it better this way too," he said gravely. "I'm apt to be a little careless with my crumbs, and you know what a state of agitation that always puts him into."

The chief steward went off looking shocked disapproval.

We ate for the most part in silence, and I was grateful that he did not try to talk. After I had had my coffee I began to feel a lot better, and the aching in my throat subsided.

I had taken the first relaxing pull on a cigarette when he raised his head suddenly and, looking straight into my eyes, said humorously, "But I still don't understand, you know, why you came into my cabin last night."

CHAPTER FIVE

I STARED AT HIM in blank astonishment. When at last I got my breath I gasped inadequately, "What!"

"Tell me all about it," he said persuasively.

"But I didn't—I didn't! I never went to your cabin. I've—I've never been in it."

His grey eyes never left my face, but they lost their twinkle and became speculative.

"Do you ever walk in your sleep?" he asked finally.

"Never," I said shortly. "I've never walked in my sleep, and I wasn't in your cabin last night. So you'll have to make up something else."

"Simple enough," he agreed, "if I'd made it up. But I didn't. Someone came into my room last night, and if it wasn't you it was wearing your dressing robe—that elegant bit of stuff you had on this morning when you let out those bloodcurdling yells."

I felt my face grow hot at his mention of my hysteria. I was feeling ashamed of it by that time, because I had always wanted to be one of those cool persons who handle an emergency with calmness and efficiency. Besides, I was beginning to resent his insistence that I had been in his cabin.

I stood up abruptly. "I can assure you, Mr. Arnold," I said coldly, "that I've never been in your room. You've made some sort of a mistake, and I think you ought to be gentleman enough to admit it."

I sailed off but spoiled the whole thing because my sleeve caught the end of a fork, and the thing went clattering to the floor. I heard the Arnold creature laugh as a steward went to pick it up, and I went out the door feeling furious and a fool at the same time.

I met Celia Merton, Mrs. Jennings and Mr. Imhoff on the stairs, and they pounced on me and started asking questions all at once.

"Who did it?" cried Celia.

"Is it true that that Mr. Arnold did it?" Mrs. Jennings wanted to know.

Mr. Imhoff said that Mr. Arnold had known Sally before they met on the boat, hadn't he?

I said no, I didn't think so, and realized that my voice sounded shocked. It had never occurred to me that Mr. Arnold might have had anything to do with it!

I brushed past them and went up on deck, where I sat down to think it over.

Perhaps he had done it. Why should I calmly assume that he had not, just because he was so—well, so darned attractive. And yet I could not make myself believe it. There was something about the man . . . If he was a murderer, then it seemed to me you could not trust anyone at all.

But why did he keep hinting that I had been in his room? Maybe if he had done it he was trying to put the blame on me as the only other person in the deluxe suite section!

The thought was so intolerable that I jumped up from my chair, all ready to do battle for my good name.

I went straight to the captain's room and rapped smartly on the door.

I was told to come in and found the captain and purser just finishing a cozy breakfast together. They stood up and eyed me gravely.

Poor Captain Lang looked almost as gloomy as Mr. Ogilvie by this time. His sunburned, jolly face had settled into lines and furrows, and the change was startling. I guessed that they found the situation somewhat above their heads.

I told them about Mr. Arnold and his preposterous accusation, and they seemed very interested. They accompanied me to my cabin, and I showed them how the chair had been moved, and then we all shifted over to Mr. Arnold's cabin, where Captain Lang stood rather helplessly in the middle of the floor, and the purser poked about aimlessly.

"It's possible, I suppose," said Mr. Ogilvie after a while, "that if both you and Mr. Arnold are telling the truth—"

"I'm telling the truth," I interrupted firmly.

"If, as I say, you are both telling the truth, someone could have entered your stateroom, picked up the dressing robe and moved the chair and then entered Mr. Arnold's stateroom, wearing the garment. But I see no reason why anyone would. Was the dressing robe lying over the chair that was moved?"

I shook my head, and he shrugged and turned away. I knew he did not believe either of us, and somehow, when he told it that way, I couldn't blame him. It all sounded absolutely silly.

I looked at them both rather helplessly and sighed, and at that moment the door opened, and Mr. Arnold walked in.

He glanced around quickly and looked last and longest at me.

"Hello," he said cheerfully. "Board meeting?"

I suppose we all felt a bit foolish. I know I did.

The purser cleared his throat. "Er—Mr. Arnold, Miss Bray tells us you thought she came into your cabin last night, and we are trying to investigate the matter."

The man actually winked at me! And then he said humorously, "Looking for footprints? Only it didn't rain last night, and the ground's pretty hard."

The captain forgot himself and smiled, but Mr. Ogilvie said sternly, "This is not a jesting matter, Mr. Arnold."

They started to question him then, and it seemed to me that he was honestly trying to tell them all he knew.

It appeared that one of the lights on the deck shone into his room, so that it was never very dark. He had seen someone, wearing my robe, bending over the washbasin. He suggested that perhaps it was washing its teeth—and drew another frown from Mr. Ogilvie.

He had not seen the head clearly at all, but part of the robe had been in the light that came from the deck, and he had seen it distinctly. Unless there were two such dressing robes on board he was willing to swear that it had been mine.

He had watched for a moment and then had given it a genial "Good evening." It gave some sort of startled movement and then glided swiftly out of the room.

"Now, Mr. Arnold," said the purser, "can you state definitely that this person was a woman?"

Mr. Arnold considered it and then shook his head. "I naturally assumed it was a woman, of course, because of the dressing gown. But it could have been a man—I did not see it clearly enough to be sure. As I say, the only thing that was quite distinct was part of the gown. Beautiful thing," he added courteously, glancing at me.

I had always thought so, too, so I smiled and said, "Thank you."

The purser almost stamped his foot.

"Mr. Arnold, did you see this person come into your room?"

"No. I woke up suddenly, and it was standing there by the basin."

The purser whispered to the captain, who nodded unhappily, and they both turned to go. As they passed through the door Mr. Ogilvie flung over his shoulder, "I have not forgotten, Mr. Arnold, that your first statement to me was that you had slept like a log all night."

He closed the door with a snap before anyone could answer him, and I burst out laughing. I couldn't help it.

"Serves you right," I said, "for going around telling lies."

He looked down at me with an odd expression. "Ingratitude," he murmured. "I lied to save your good name."

I stood up. "Do you mean to say you still think—"

"No. I believe you. It was not you last night. But it is this morning."

"But—"

"It would not be fair to you," he said reasonably, "to let the opportunity pass. Not to me, either, of course."

"What on earth . . . ?"

"Look at it this way. When you're telling this tale to some girl friend, later on, you say, 'And then the captain and the purser went out and calmly left me there in his cabin—with him.' "

"I'm going," I said indignantly.

He laid a firm hand on my shoulder.

"Naturally the girl friend says 'And what happened then?'—rather breathlessly, I should think. You can't say, 'Nothing,' you know. Come to think of it, it wouldn't even be fair to the girl friend."

I gasped and tried to free my shoulder, but I couldn't. I'm willing to swear I couldn't. He simply put his arm around me and bent my head back and kissed me on the mouth—twice. And I did try to stop him.

As soon as he let me go I walked straight out of his cabin without a word.

CHAPTER SIX

I WENT BACK to my cabin, determined to get a much needed nap. I took off my dress but for some reason recoiled from the famous dressing gown and dug another one out of my trunk instead.

I lay down, but for a while I was restless. When at last I realized that it was not poor Sally's death that was disturbing me but Mr. Arnold's kisses, I called myself six kinds of a fool and forced my mind to a state of blankness.

I got off all right then and slept soundly until just before lunch, when I was awakened by a knock on the door. I called, "Come," drowsily, and Chet burst in, looking wild and disheveled.

"Carla," he said tragically. "You must have heard something last night. Why, it was—right next to you! Can't you think of anything? I've got to find out who did this. I'll get him if it's the last thing I do!"

I sat up and pushed my hair back from my face.

"I don't see what you can do, Chet," I said mildly. "I'm sure everything possible is being done."

"Oh hell!" he said savagely. "That long-nosed fool Ogilvie'll never find anything. He's too dumb."

I wanted to laugh, but I knew poor Chet would be hurt. He was so terribly in earnest—and so terribly unhappy. I was sorry about it, and I knew that he'd never have had a chance with Sally anyway. He'd never know that now, though.

The luncheon bugle went, and I pushed him out while I dressed.

Everyone was down at lunch, including even Captain Lang and our star detective, Mr. Ogilvie. There was a continuous low buzz of conversation.

I noticed at once—and with more annoyance than I could account for—that Mr. Arnold was seated at the captain's table. I knew perfectly well that he could have stayed at my table if he had wanted to, and I felt my chin go up a couple of inches.

It was obvious, even from where I sat, that the Marsh girls were tickled pink. Their plain faces were alive and animated, and they talked almost continuously. I didn't blame them, poor things, but when it dawned on me that Lady Marsh was actually throwing her weight about and trying to get Mr. Arnold for herself I felt almost sick. "Mean old hag," I thought bitterly. "It's like taking candy front a baby to outshine Lucy and Phyllis. She's a bitch."

It was pretty gloomy at our table. Sally had always been so gay and noisy. And Chet would keep asking questions about how she had died.

Dr. Barton was patient with him, although I'm sure he would have preferred to talk about something else.

At Chet's insistence he explained for the third time: "She died almost at once. She was standing on the chair, and apparently it was jerked from under her. Her neck was broken. The length of the cord—"

"Yes, but—but, good God!" Chet clutched at his unruly hair with a wild hand. "What would she be doing standing on a chair while somebody put a noose around her neck?"

The doctor shrugged. "I wish we knew. It's strange that the cord should have cut her so."

"Well, I'll tell you one thing," I said thoughtfully. "It must have been some sort of a joke—I mean, I guess Sally was supposed to think it was a joke, because I distinctly heard her giggle."

"You heard her giggle?" Chet shouted. "Where? Where?"

I had to go over it all again, twice, for him, after which he left his lunch and rushed off to confer with the captain and the purser, much as he disliked their methods.

The afternoon was spent in endless discussions, and theories of all kinds were put forth. Everybody took part, and the captain and purser were chased all over the ship by willing helpers.

Just before dinner Kay, Peter and I retired to the smoke room and ordered cocktails. We wanted to get away from it all, but it wasn't long before everybody but Mrs. Jennings and Mr. Arnold had trailed in after us and were sitting around us in one big circle.

Mrs. Jennings had not come, because she never entered the smoke room on principle, and we discovered afterward that she had been intensely annoyed and deeply offended because we had not congregated in the drawing room with her. Mr. Arnold had not been seen by anyone for about two hours.

Since he was not with us, someone suggested that he might be the murderer, and Chet pounced on the idea and got quite excited about it. He lowered his voice and said that Mr. Arnold might be a rejected suitor of Sally's mother, who was reputed to be a great beauty, and so had taken his revenge by murdering her daughter.

Lady Marsh and Mr. Imhoff said together and very loudly, "Rubbish!" and at that moment Mr. Arnold stepped into the room and wanted to know what was rubbish.

We couldn't tell him, of course, and we all sat there feeling rather silly.

He looked at us for a moment and then told us that the dinner bugle had gone so long ago that the captain had sent him up to see what was wrong.

We all trooped down and were joined by Mrs. Jennings, who apparently had not heard the bugle either, on the stairway. She walked down with us and yet made us feel, somehow, that she was no part of us.

When we got to the dining saloon we discovered that the bugle had not been blown and we were ahead of time. The stewards were somewhat disconcerted and tried to hint that we all go up again, but we refused. Peter said maybe we'd get our soup hot for a change.

Sir Alfred was furious. "What the devil do you mean, sir," he bellowed at Mr. Arnold, "by telling us the bugle had blown and the captain sent you up for us?"

Mr. Arnold raised his eyebrows and stared coldly. "The sight of a dozen people tongue-tied with embarrassment because they had just been discussing me as a possible murderer was too much for my gentle nature. So I reached out a helping hand."

CHAPTER SEVEN

AFTER DINNER that evening I felt my first qualm about the coming night. During the bright sunshine of the day I had not thought about it, somehow, but with the coming of darkness I began to feel frightened and nervous. I dreaded the thought of going to bed, and at last I decided to try and get up a bridge game. I thought if I played late I might get tired enough to go straight to sleep.

Celia Merton and Mr. Imhoff readily agreed to play. They were both good players and were both a little annoyed when we were finally obliged to fall back on Phyllis Marsh for a fourth.

Phyllis, as everybody knew, was a foul bridge player, and I decided to take her for my partner in order to keep the peace. I knew if she played with either of the others they would criticize everything she did and make her so nervous that she wouldn't know one card from another.

As we sat down I made a firm resolution that she could trump every ace I held and I would not say a word or get annoyed. I kept to it pretty well, too, except for one time when she led the only wrong card there was to lead, and I found myself clicking my teeth.

Kay was obviously delighted when she saw me settling down to bridge, and somehow it disgusted me a little to see her dashing right along with her man hunt. It seemed to me that she could have sat back and stayed quiet for a day or two after what had happened. And the rest would have done her good.

However, she soon had Peter and Robert Arnold sitting at a table with her, drinking something.

I was absorbed in the game for a hand, and the next time I looked Mr. Arnold had disappeared, and Sir Alfred and Lady Marsh and Lucy were sitting there instead. Kay looked glum.

"Serves her right," I thought grimly. "She ought to relax once in a while, and she'd do better." I reflected further that it must be a good deal of a strain to have to strive constantly to be seen only with men.

It was at this point that Phyllis' super-foul lead hit my consciousness, and I clicked my teeth.

After a time I could feel that someone was standing behind my chair, and he presently began to make little clicking sounds of dismay every time I played a card. I turned my head sharply and knew, even before I met his cool grey eyes, that it was Robert Arnold.

I said coldly, "Would you prefer to play the hand yourself?"

He laughed down at me and shook his head. "Oh no—no. I've seen all the other hands. Thought I'd give you a hint."

Mr. Imhoff lost his temper suddenly and completely and threw his hand onto the table. "That's not fair!" he shouted.

"If I'm not wanted, of course," said Mr. Arnold in a hurt voice, "I'll go."

Celia Merton looked uncomfortable and distressed.

"Oh, don't take it that way, Mr. Arnold," she said. "I'm sure it wasn't meant that way."

I longed to tell her not to be an ass.

Phyllis said, "Go and talk to Lucy, Mr. Arnold. She's quite alone."

I looked up and saw that Lucy was quite alone. Kay and Peter and the elder Marshes had disappeared, and she sat at the table lately occupied by therm, drooping thinly and doing absolutely nothing.

Mr. Arnold sauntered off and sat down by her, and our game went on quietly, without further interruption.

I glanced from time to time at Lucy and Mr. Arnold, and every time I looked he was talking volubly and Lucy was listening with her mouth hanging slightly open and an expression of utter astonishment on her face.

Once the purser came in and walked slowly around as though looking for someone or something and then went out again without saying anything.

By half-past twelve I was very tired, and when the rubber was finished I suggested that we stop. Celia and Mr. Imhoff were more than ready—it was long past bedtime for them, anyway—but Phyllis, for some reason, wanted to go on.

However, we took no notice of her, as people seldom did, and counted up, and of course she and I had lost.

As we left, Lucy and Mr. Arnold stood up, too, and followed us down. I think Lucy would have been well pleased to sit there and listen all night, but Mr. Arnold propelled her to the door with a firm hand on her elbow.

As we came to my deck Celia Merton said, "I wonder if the body is still in that stateroom? I should think it probably is, don't you? I mean, I don't suppose there's any other place for it."

I stood perfectly still and watched her and Mr. Imhoff as they went on down the stairs. I felt faintly sick and was suddenly quite wide awake again.

"All that bridge playing—and putting up with Phyllis—for nothing," I thought bitterly.

And then Robert Arnold had me by the arm, and we were walking along the passage to our cabins.

"Really, you know," he said conversationally, "you shouldn't keep me up so late."

"Keep you up?" I cried indignantly. "I didn't."

"I can't let you come along this corridor alone at night," he explained patiently.

"Oh, rubbish!" I said rather feebly. "Why not?"

"Because things have been happening around these lonely outlying suburbs."

He opened my door for me and then calmly walked in after and methodically searched the cabin and the bathroom as well. I sat on the bed and watched him with raised eyebrows.

When he finished with the bathroom he went to the window and, adjusting it so that it was half open, took a small pair of pincers from his pocket and screwed the bolt tight.

"Now," he said, turning to me, "no one can get in there. The other bathroom door is locked on the inside, and if you lock this door after I go out nobody will be able to get in—not even me."

I smiled faintly and felt that I ought to be civil enough to thank him for the trouble he'd taken.

I opened my mouth to say something polite, but before I could get it out he bent over and kissed me chastely on the forehead and said airily, "Good night, my dear," and went out, closing the door behind him.

I forgot my impulse to be civil and hated him afresh. The kiss had been so casual! I felt angrily that either he should kiss me as though he meant it—or not at all!

As I undressed I thought of several cutting things I might have said to him, and I tried them out loud, because the silence had suddenly become oppressive and frightening.

I had just finished declaiming, "Why don't you go back to Tahiti, where you are probably a riot with the natives?" when I heard the door open behind me and spun around with a stifled scream. It was Robert Arnold again.

"Are you alone?" he asked anxiously and, before I could reply, stepped into the bathroom to see for himself.

I clutched my dressing gown around me and prepared to say one of the cutting things, but as usual he butted in first.

"Phew! That gave me a fright. I thought someone was in here with you—that's why I came in without knocking—and gave you a fright. Serves you right too. And why didn't you lock the door?"

He actually waited for me to answer, and with this opportunity to say all the cutting things I had practiced I got flustered, couldn't remember one of them and botched it completely.

I said helplessly, "Is that so?"

"Inadequate, Carla. And you haven't answered my question."

"I'm not going to answer it," I said fiercely. "Who told you my name?"

"A dear old soul by the name of Jennings. I asked her. I told her I was thinking of proposing to you —don't get excited, because I haven't quite made up my mind yet—and I thought it would go over better if I knew your first name. The Jennings gave it up reluctantly and passed the remark that her daughter made the best jam tarts in all Australia."

"Disastrous for me," I murmured scornfully. "A rival. I can't make jam tarts."

"I might overlook that. Anyway, don't be jealous." He went over to the window and picked up the pincers. "I found I'd left these behind; that's why I came back. And this time lock the door—unless you aim to get yourself strangled. Good night."

He went out, leaving me with several good answers that had to go to waste.

CHAPTER EIGHT

I LOCKED THE DOOR after Mr. Arnold and then got into bed and turned off the light. I told myself that with the two doors locked on the inside and the window fastened securely everything would be all right and I would drop off to sleep at once.

I must have told myself the same thing about a dozen times in the next hour, but it didn't do any good. I couldn't sleep. I kept remembering Celia Merton's remark about Sally being still in the next room. Only I couldn't think of it as being just poor Sally lying dead—it seemed like some monstrous horror in there, only separated from me by a bathroom door.

I had some moments of anger to think that they would leave her there, and for a while I thought of ringing for the steward and complaining about it. But further thought convinced me that it would be useless. After all, he would not be able to do anything about it; he could only say that he was sorry and would probably sneer respectfully while saying it. And yet if I had rung for him when the impulse was on me I would have saved myself a lot of trouble.

I tossed and turned and kept raising my head to make sure that no one was looking in the window. There are all sorts of noises on a ship, and any one that I could not immediately place raised a fresh alarm in my troubled mind. At last I took myself sternly in hand and resolved to ignore all further noises, no matter what they sounded like.

That worked pretty well, and after a while I fell into a doze. I don't know how long it lasted, but suddenly I was wide awake again, my heart pounding and my ears straining for a repetition of whatever sound had awakened me. But there was only the usual dull throb of the engines, creaking of wood and swish of water.

I lay there for a while, but nothing happened, and I realized that my feet and hands were cold and I was shaking and trembling senselessly. I called myself a fool and decided to get up and bathe my face in cold water.

I switched on the reading light over the bed and went into the darkened bathroom. As I felt for the switch I distinctly heard a sound in the next cabin where that horrid thing lay.

My hand fell to my side, and I don't think I breathed for a moment. The sound was that of soft footsteps, and I had a nightmare vision of

Sally's corpse moving restlessly about in search of revenge.

The next instant the door to my bathroom was tried. The knob turned slowly in the semidarkness, and the door was pushed. When it did not give the knob was released, and after a silent moment the footsteps seemed to retreat across the room, and I heard the click of a closing door.

I stumbled back into my cabin, my breath coming in sobbing gasps. I remember whispering to myself, "I'm locked in. It can't get in to me—it can't." And then I thought of the steward and turned, with a frightened whimper, to press the bell.

I never rang it, for at that instant I heard soft footsteps coming down the corridor to my door. I stood frozen to the spot, my eyes stretched and staring.

I watched the knob turn slowly—twice—and although I knew the door was locked I had some sort of fearful idea that the thing would be able to come through anyway.

The door and everything else dissolved into a grey mist, and I shrieked wildly until blackness closed over me.

I guess I wasn't out for long, because the next thing I remember I was lying on the floor and seeing Robert Arnold at the window, desperately trying to unscrew the bolt he'd fastened so securely a few hours earlier.

I got up dizzily, holding onto the washbasin, and became conscious of a babble of voices outside my door.

The Arnold man called through the window, "Carla! Are you all right?"

"I don't know," I said weakly and began to cry.

"Open the door. I'm coming round," he said peremptorily and disappeared.

I unlocked the door, and Mr. Ogilvie, two stewards and a stewardess poured in. I think they were faintly disappointed that there was no bloody corpse.

Mr. Ogilvie cleared his throat and asked formally, "What is the trouble, Miss Bray?"

Mr. Arnold added himself to the crowd, and I suddenly felt a bit foolish. But I raised my chin and told them everything. And when it seemed, somehow, a bit inadequate, I added that I had been nervous anyway, what with the corpse lying in the next room.

"But it isn't," said Mr. Ogilvie tartly. "Why should you think that? Of course we had it removed today."

I said, "Oh," rather feebly, and Robert Arnold turned to the purser and said, "You'll have to leave a steward on guard in this hall all night.

Perhaps you'll find out who's trying to get into this room, that way. But in any case I think it's necessary."

Mr. Ogilvie said impatiently, "I'll tell the night watchman to keep a sharp lookout." He turned to me. "Are you all right now, Miss Bray?"

"Quite all right," I replied, trying not to cry again.

"I'll want to question you in the morning. I don't think you'll be disturbed again tonight." He backed out and took his stooges with him, and I was left alone again with the Arnold man.

He walked over to the window and said absently, "Well, I'll have to make the rounds again. I wasn't able to get in the window myself, even with my pincers, and, as has been demonstrated, the doors are fast. So I think old Ogilvie is right for once and you won't be disturbed again."

I felt suddenly that I could not be in that cabin alone, that I wanted to cry out and beg him to stay with me for the rest of the night, but of course I couldn't—and anyway, I wouldn't have given him the satisfaction.

I pulled myself together and said with as much dignity as I could command, "I'm perfectly all right now, and I'm sure nothing more will happen. It was Celia Merton's fault anyway, saying she thought they'd left Sally lying in there. Naturally I was upset when I heard footsteps."

He looked down at note oddly and murmured, "That's funny. Can't understand, you know, why she should have said that. Because she was an interested spectator when they took the body away."

CHAPTER NINE

THE NEXT MORNING, seemed to know about my experience, and I felt as though I had been headlined in a newspaper. I was asked again and again to tell the whole story from beginning to end, and I got so embarrassed and so tired of it that at last I hid in the drawing room with a book.

The book was mere camouflage, for I could not get my mind off Sally and everything that had happened. I had been fond of her and I was very anxious to see the mystery cleared up and her murderer punished. And I had less than no confidence in Mr. Ogilvie.

I thought about it for a while and suddenly remembered Celia Merton. Robert Arnold had said that she knew perfectly well the body had been removed when she made the remark that kept me awake all night.

I decided to do a little investigating of my own and started out in search of her.

I found her on the boat deck playing shuffleboard with Mr. Imhoff.

She did not seem to want to be disturbed, but I disturbed her anyhow. I took her to one side and asked her straight out why she had suggested that the corpse was still in the cabin next to me when she knew perfectly well that it was not.

She appeared embarrassed, gave a silly laugh and after a glance of modesty at Mr. Imhoff wiggled and pulled her girdle down a bit.

"Mr. Condit told me to do it," she said with a faint simper. "We thought it would be a joke."

"Damn funny," I agreed bitterly. "And it worked beautifully, didn't it?"

She got very red in the face, then, and muttered, "I'm sorry," and I turned my back on her and walked away.

I thought grimly, "Yes. If the great Mr. Peter Hothouse Condit had told Celia to jump overboard she would have done it gladly. Her ambition could go no higher than to be an accepted sophisticate!"

I went straight after Peter and tracked him down on the promenade deck. He was draped artistically over the rail and looked very elegant and very languid. He gave me a nice smile.

I frowned by way of return and asked him point-blank why he had told Celia to play such a silly joke.

He sighed and said frankly, "Because I was bored—and I thought you probably were bored too. And it seemed to me that a corpse in the next cabin might be stimulating no end."

"So it was," I said coldly. "And not only was I stimulated, I was terrified as well."

"Better to be terrified than bored," he murmured.

I was furious. "That may be the way you feel," I told him, "but as far as I'm concerned there's nothing I'd rather be, right this minute, than thoroughly bored. And I'd thank you—"

"Yes, I know," he said pacifically. "But let's go and have a drink. I've been a naughty boy, and I'm sorry, and it won't ever happen again. Come along."

He took my arm and urged me along to the smoke room, where he sat me down and proceeded to order some sherry.

We sipped the wine and talked for a while, and then a steward came up and said that the purser wanted to see me in his office.

I rose reluctantly, for I knew I'd have to tell my story all over again, and I was getting very tired of it.

When I got there I found that Kay Bayliss and Mrs. Jennings were also there. Mrs. Jennings was red in the face and seemed to be angry about something. Kay was wearing her amused expression.

Mr. Ogilvie waved me to a seat and turned back to what had evidently been an interrupted conversation with Mrs. Jennings.

"Now you say you heard Miss Grable talking to someone in the corridor near your cabin, but you don't know to whom she was talking?"

I really admired the man. Anyone else would have said, "You don't know who she was talking to?"

Mrs. Jennings said firmly, "No, I do not. The other voice was just an indistinct murmur—and then they passed on."

"Did they go in the direction of Miss Grable's cabin?"

"No—they went towards the stairway."

"Then," said Mr. Ogilvie in dour triumph, "it was probably the murderer to whom she was talking."

"Not necessarily," I suggested brightly.

He flung me an unclear look and returned to Mrs. Jennings.

"Now can't you possibly tell me whether she was with a man or a woman?"

"I cannot," said Mrs. Jennings with dignity. "I listened carefully at the time, because I rather disapproved of her wandering about the corridors at that time of night—but it was impossible to tell."

"And have you no idea of the time?" the purser almost pleaded.

"No, I have not. I know only that I had been asleep and that I woke up. I went to sleep again when they went away."

"And have you no idea of the time you heard her over your side?" he asked, turning suddenly to Kay.

She had been studying her scarlet fingernails in a bored fashion, and she raised her eyes and said lazily, "No. I had been reading, and it must have been half an hour to an hour after the time we came down to go to bed."

Mr. Ogilvie pounced, like a dog onto a bone. "What time did you go down to bed?"

"I don't know," said Kay annoyingly, and he frowned in impatience.

"Surely you must have some idea," he said crossly.

"Well, yes. It was somewhere between eleven and one."

Mr. Ogilvie struggled in silence with his temper for a space.

"I think it was around twelve," I said, resisting an impulse to put up my hand and ask for permission before speaking.

He fixed me with a piercing look and said curtly, "I shall question you later."

I subsided, and he turned back to Kay.

"Then you say it was some time after that that you heard her walk along the corridor near you? Now how do you know that it was Miss Grable?"

"Two reasons," said Kay readily. "One was her walk—I couldn't mistake that—and the other was that she cleared her throat as she passed—and I couldn't mistake that either."

I remembered the funny, peremptory little way Sally used to clear her throat, and I knew that Kay was right. You couldn't miss it.

Mr. Ogilvie nodded. "And you say she was walking away from the stairway, up the corridor towards the other cabins?"

Kay nodded, and I mentally marked down the people who had cabins up that way. Mr. Imhoff, Peter Condit and Celia Merton.

The purser rose, ushered out Kay and Mrs. Jennings and turned his attention to me.

As I had anticipated, I had to go minutely over the details of the night before, and after that was over I was ushered out too.

It was nearly lunch time, so I went on down to my cabin to wash up a bit. I was thinking of Celia and Peter, and suddenly, and quite definitely, I knew that Peter Condit had never played that practical joke on me. In the first place he loathed practical joking—it was in character that he should —and in any case he had often expressed his scorn and contempt for it. Secondly, throughout the voyage he had never been known to do anything of the sort.

No, he had not done it as a joke. He must have done it because it was necessary—and grimly necessary—unless he had completely changed his personality overnight.

But why? What earthly reason could there have been? It didn't make sense. Of what help could it have been to Peter Condit for me to be frightened half out of my wits?

I was aroused from these reflections by a push from behind, and the Arnold man said cheerfully, "Why don't you look where you're going?"

He took my arm and led me to my cabin. I opened the door and he calmly followed me in and seated himself on a chair.

"Do you think it's quite decent to spend so much time in my cabin?" I asked mildly. "People might talk."

He grinned at me. "I don't think anyone has found out about it yet, and of course if they do I'll have to marry you—noblesse oblige and all that; but now, to business. Let's hear all about the conference in the purser's wigwam."

I went to the mirror and started to fix my face. "What do you want to know for?" I asked carelessly.

"I want to tell Mr. Imhoff—he's dying of curiosity."

"Let him die."

He dropped his banter and said persuasively, "Please, Carla. I have something to tell you if you'll come across."

That got me of course. But I insisted that he wait until teatime. The luncheon bugle had gone, and I told him that I had to have a nap after lunch. "I have to do my sleeping in the daytime," I explained, "because it seems to be impossible to get any at night. But I'll meet you for tea, and I promise to talk then."

He agreed readily enough and said that he'd take a nap too. "I don't get much sleep at night either, you know," he said airily. "There's a woman in my section who's always screaming."

I threw a book at him, and he departed hastily.

CHAPTER TEN

I HAD A LONG SLEEP after lunch and woke up just in time to dress for tea. I found myself putting on my prettiest dress and was annoyed about it— but not to the extent of taking it off again.

I met Robert on the veranda, and we found a small table for two, where we hoped not to be interrupted.

He got out of me everything that had transpired in the purser's office, and he seemed very interested.

"Then it seems," he mused, "that poor little Sally walked over from her side of the ship to Kay's side some time after she went to her cabin, and then went past Kay's cabin, presumably to visit Celia Merton, Mr. Imhoff or Peter Condit."

"Peter," I said briefly.

"Why?"

"If you'd known Sally as I did you'd understand. She certainly would not have bothered to visit either Celia or Mr. Imhoff for any reason."

"Oh. All right, Peter then. After her visit to him she must have gone back to her own cabin, since she would not have passed Mrs. Jennings' cabin if she had gone straight upstairs. Now either Peter accompanied her, or she had met someone else when she started for the stairs."

I thought it over for a while in silence, and then I whispered wretchedly, "Good Lord! Do you suppose Peter did it?"

He laughed at me. "Now you're jumping to conclusions. Remember, we haven't any evidence to show that it was he she visited."

"I know, but I feel sure of it. And anyway, there's—there's something funny about Peter."

"What do you mean?" he asked sharply.

I told him all about the practical joke and how it could not have been a practical joke—and felt uncomfortable and disloyal, because I had known Peter for two weeks and Robert for only two days.

Robert said slowly, "That's strange. There doesn't seem to be any reason for it."

"There must be," I insisted. "Peter's vanity would never allow him to do anything so gauche without a very good reason. I know that."

"Well . . ." He extricated his long legs from the little wicker table.

"Let's go and talk to him and see if we can find out anything. Where does he usually hang out at this time of day?"

"Smoke room," I said laconically. "He's always there."

"Come along. We'll buy him a drink if we have to."

He took my arm, and we moved off down the deck. The sun was low in the sky, and the sea was dark blue, with a faint sparkle. I felt suddenly that I didn't want to go to the smoke room and start gnawing on the horrid problem all over again. I wanted to walk on around the deck with Robert and, presently, to lean on the rail and watch the sunset.

But apparently Robert had no thought but to talk to Peter, for he marched me straight to the smoke room without any dallying.

Peter was sitting with Kay, and they were both slumped down in their chairs and seemed to be staring at their respective drinks. They looked deathly bored, and they both brightened up noticeably as we approached.

We sat down with them, and Robert ordered drinks, and then to my amazement he ignored the murder completely and began to talk about Tahiti instead. He made it quite interesting, and it was not long before he had us all arguing about whether the water in the harbor was royal blue or turquoise.

When we were in the heat of it he suddenly switched us to women. He said the colors of the harbor at Tahiti reminded him of different women. "The royal blue," he declared, "is the sophisticated woman, whereas the turquoise is like the young girl—shallow, gay, pretty—"

I giggled, and he promptly kicked me under the table.

Peter took it up seriously. "Now I disagree with you. To me the sophisticated woman is the turquoise—hard, shallow, witty—and the softness and beauty of the royal blue is the—er—soul of the young girl."

Kay swallowed a yawn and said, "It's time to dress for dinner. Let's meet for cocktails, and we can finish the discussion then."

"Right," agreed Robert. "I invite you all to cocktails—my party."

The conclave broke up, and Robert and I made our way towards our deluxe cabins.

I felt that the whole thing had been a flop, and I said scornfully, "I suppose you are all ready, now, to name the murderer."

"Overlooking the sarcasm," said Robert equably, "I found out what I wanted to."

"You mean that the water at Tahiti—"

"Don't interrupt," he said sternly. "I discovered that Mr. Condit, for all his sophistication, still prefers gay youth. Of you three women—you and Kay and Sally—you know, I suspect he liked Sally the best. In any case he prefers young, untouched girls, as those super sophisticates often do—for reasons best known to themselves."

"Do you mean to tell me you talked all that rubbish about Tahiti just to find out that?" I asked in surprise.

He nodded.

"Well, why didn't you just ask him and save time?"

"I prefer the subtle way," he said loftily. "And as for the time element—we have a week yet, and there's plenty of it."

I sniffed. "While you're playing so fast and loose with time don't forget that Mr. Ogilvie is working on the thing too. It would be too bad if he solved it first!"

I went on into my cabin and turned on the water in the bath. I undressed and took a dressing gown from the wardrobe—the one I had worn when Sally was discovered and that Robert swore had been in his cabin. I put it on and, as I did so, noticed there was a handkerchief in the pocket. I stepped towards the laundry bag to put it in, but as I pulled it out of the pocket something fell from it and clattered to the floor. I stooped over and picked it up. It was a ring—a signet ring belonging to Peter Condit.

CHAPTER ELEVEN

I STARED AT THE THING in amazement. How on earth could Peter's ring have found its way into the pocket of my dressing gown? And it must have been there on the morning we discovered poor Sally, for I had not used it since.

I dressed hastily and went along to Robert's cabin with the thing clutched in my hand. I knocked at the door, and at the same time a steward passed by and made an elaborate business of not seeing me. I felt that he was thinking, "If only young ladies would not go around knocking on young gentlemen's doors," and I muttered, "Damn all stewards!"

Robert opened the door and bowed me in. He was in his shirt sleeves.

"So nice of you," he said with a flourish. "You can help me finish dressing."

"Stop being smart," I said shortly. "It's as much as I can do to dress myself without dressing you too. I came here to show you something."

I opened my hand and disclosed the ring, and he stopped dressing entirely and stared at it.

I told him where it had come from, and he said slowly, "Then it would seem that on the night of the murder Peter Condit went into your room, put on your dressing gown, came along into my room for a bit, then took the ring off his finger and dropped it into the pocket of the dressing gown, went back to your room and returned dressing gown, complete with ring."

I laughed at him. "It sounds madder than the hatter's tea party. And the idea of Peter putting on a girl's negligee is the maddest part of all. In fact, I think it's quite impossible."

I don't think he listened to me. He was silent for a moment, and then he said thoughtfully, "I suppose we ought to go to the purser with this information."

"I hate to," I said with my eyes on his face.

"So do I. He'll probably have poor Peter in irons. But it really must be done, you know."

"Why?" I asked simply.

"Because, as things stand, Ogilvie, our human bloodhound, thinks that you did it."

I stared at him. "He thinks *I* did it?"

"Why not?" said Robert reasonably. "He has no one else to suspect."

"What about you?" I cried hotly.

"Well—technically. But I have such an honest face that of course he—"

"Oh, shut up," I said wearily. "Let's go and have our cocktails. We can think it over for a while before we tell the purser. Maybe we can figure out some explanation."

"Half a minute. You wouldn't dress me, so I'll have to do it myself."

He put on his coat and did one or two other things, and then he patted his hair and said, "Now! Am I pretty?"

"Sweet," I replied and walked out of the cabin.

He followed me, calling in a stage whisper, "Did you look up and down the corridor first to make I sure no one saw us?"

I ignored him, and we went on up to the smoke room.

Kay and Peter were already there, and Kay said sweetly, "Oh, you both finished dressing at the same time."

I felt my face grow hot, and I wanted to slap her, but Robert said easily, "No, we didn't. Carla beat me by fifteen minutes—but she cheated. She didn't wash behind the ears."

Peter laughed, but Kay turned her eyes away with a sullen expression. Robert ordered drinks, and we settled down.

We talked aimlessly for a while, and then Robert threw a bombshell—although he spoke casually enough.

He said, "I suppose, Mr. Condit, that this tragedy was a great blow to you?"

Peter threw up his head like a startled horse. "Why?" he asked sharply.

"I understand you and Sally were engaged."

"What!" Peter almost shouted. "Engaged? Ridiculous! Where on earth did you get such an idea?"

It occurred to me, foggily and somehow uncomfortably, that Peter was protesting too much. I saw Kay give him a curious glance.

"Oh—sorry," Robert murmured smoothly. "I must have got it wrong. But I thought I saw her with your ring."

There was an uneasy pause while Peter fingered his glass in confusion. Then, suddenly, he pushed the glass away and leaned back in his chair.

"She might have had it for all I know," he said easily. "I lost the damn thing several days ago."

There was another silence, which Robert broke to order more cocktails.

I was thinking furiously. If Robert had seen Sally wearing the ring, how could he possibly have known that it belonged to Peter Condit?

He had only just met us all and had merely seen Sally for a short time in the smoke room before he went off to bed.

I wondered if Peter had thought of that and glanced at him, but his face was blank.

I fell into thought again. If Sally had worn it in the smoke room that night . . . And then I remembered: Peter had worn his ring all day when we went ashore at Tahiti.

And so, of course, Robert could not have seen it on Sally, since he had gone off to bed as soon as Peter and I came in.

CHAPTER TWELVE

THAT NIGHT—the second after Sally's death—the purser announced that the orchestra would play on the deck for dancing. We understood that the idea had been the captain's, and the object was to cheer us up. I believe the purser disapproved of it wholeheartedly.

The prospect of a dance made me shudder. We'd had them every few days, all the way from Sydney, of course, but there were too few of us for it to be any good. The only time we'd really had fun was the fancy-dress ball, when the second class had been invited up.

Nobody was much cheered except the Marsh girls. They were always pleased when a dance was announced—although, as far as I could see, they invariably had a miserable time. I suppose they went on hoping for a break, because they were always eager and excited right up to the time they were left sitting against the wall.

It all goes to show, too, that you should never give up—like Bruce and the spider, or was it Alfred and the cakes? Because Robert Arnold deliberately danced those girls around until he must have been exhausted. And I suppose business always brings business, because Chet gave them several dances instead of the one each that he'd been giving them all the way across. Dr. Barton rose to the fore and *actually cut in on them*—which was quite unprecedented, because he had limited them strictly to one duty dance each heretofore. The biggest surprise, however, was when I saw Peter giving Lucy a dance. It was a big night in the Marsh girls' lives.

Mr. Ogilvie never danced, but I saw him scowling from a doorway once, as though the whole thing were against his better judgment.

Celia Merton did not dance well, and she knew it. She sat and smoked cigarettes. She was not much of a smoker at other times, but she usually spread a few butts around the deck during the dances. She did an occasional turn with Mr. Imhoff, and sometimes one of the officers would feel it his duty to steer her around.

Mrs. Jennings always sat in full view of everybody and watched carefully for any irregularity, until her bedtime. Her bedtime was any hour she chose to make it, but she always spoke of it as though it were a fixed time.

Sir Alfred and Lady Marsh usually had one dance together after which he would depart to the smoke room to do his evening drinking. Lady Marsh would proceed to try and cut out her daughters in the matter of getting partners, but she never got very far.

This evening she got nowhere at all, and she was plainly furious. She went off early after telling the girls, rather acidly, not to stay up too late. I don't think they heard her at all. Their faces were flushed and their eyes sparkled, and I'd never before seen them so close to looking pretty.

Kay and I spent most of the evening with Peter and Dr. Barton. I believe I was as furious as Lady Marsh. Robert deigned to dance with me twice, and I circled around with him in cold silence.

Towards the end of the second dance he lowered his head and whispered to me, "Don't dance so close to me—Lucy might notice."

I could not help laughing, and I glanced over to where Lucy was talking animatedly with Dr. Barton, Phyllis and Chet. Dr. Barton wore his professional listening attitude, while Phyllis actually had her arm through Chet's.

"I'll be more careful," I said primly. "You're a newcomer, and naturally you want to get in with the right people. Only you shouldn't get off on the wrong foot by telling obvious lies."

He raised his eyebrows. "Fighting words," he murmured. "Lies, you say?"

"Well—lie. I know it was impossible for you to have seen Peter's ring on Sally."

"Oh, that." He tried several difficult steps, which he could not quite master. "Of course I didn't see the ring on Sally," he admitted when he had got his breath back. "That kind of lie is all in the interest of scientific deduction."

"Not bad—as excuses go," I said lightly as the orchestra wailed to a stop.

I did not see him again for some time. Kay, Peter, Dr. Barton and I went off to the smoke room and settled down to some heavy drinking. I rarely went in for drinking on a large scale, but I seemed to want to that night, and I let myself go.

Kay, Peter and I started out with gay spirits and a lot of nonsense. Dr. Barton was a little sulky because he had invited us down to his cabin, where he could have got drunk along with us, and we had refused. We did not seem to like cabins much any more.

Celia Merton and Mr. Imhoff came in for a few minutes and had a drink each in comparative silence, and then they went off—presumably to bed.

Mrs. Jennings peered in the window twice, to see how we were getting on. The second time we cheered her—but she seemed to think we were inviting her in, for she shook her head vigorously and disappeared again.

Lady Marsh came in and joined her husband, who was still sitting in his favorite corner. She was very put out because the bar had just closed and she could not get the glass of port she usually took before going to bed. She satisfied herself by drinking the remains of Sir Alfred's last whisky and soda.

Robert appeared shortly afterward with a Marsh girl on each arm—and I was drunk enough to be angry about it. I immediately became noisier and gayer.

They came straight over to our table, and Robert seated the girls and then himself. He called for drinks, and when the steward explained that the bar was closed he laughed and observed that Lucy would have to go to bed sober for once. Phyllis and Lucy giggled hysterically, but Lady Marsh reared her head and called across the room, "My girls have never been drunk, Mr. Arnold."

I realized very suddenly and very definitely that I was drunk and that I would have to go to bed at once if I were to go unassisted. I remember thinking dazedly that I didn't care what happened during the night—I'd be sure to sleep through it all.

I got up unsteadily, banged my open hand on the table and said firmly, "I'm going to bed."

They all looked at me for a minute, and then Kay struggled to her feet, put her arm through mine and announced, "Me too!"

That seemed to break up the party, and we all straggled out of the smoke room together.

When I got to my deck I discovered that Kay was still hanging onto my arm. I peered at her mistily and said politely, "I don't think you live here."

She tightened her hold on my arm. "I'm going to sleep with you tonight; I'm afraid to sleep in my own cabin."

It sounded reasonable to me, so I nodded gravely, and we started down the corridor.

We had not wavered three steps when Robert's voice spoke up sharply behind us. "No," he said, "I think it would be much better, Mrs. Bayliss, if you went to your own cabin."

I suddenly became unreasonably annoyed with Robert Arnold, and momentarily it seemed to steady me. I turned around and spoke coldly and with surprising clearness.

"Isn't it about time, Mr. Arnold, that you stopped interfering in my affairs? It has become extremely distasteful to me."

Even in my stupor I saw his eyes go wintry and remote. The line of his jaw appeared, and he looked at me for a moment in silence. Then he bowed stiffly and went into his cabin.

I felt a miserable impulse to call after him not to mind anything I said—I was extremely drunk.

Kay tugged at my arm, and I went on with her blinking through a sudden film of tears.

We pulled off our clothes and fell into bed, and the last thing I remember noticing was that Kay had borrowed my most precious nightgown.

CHAPTER THIRTEEN

I SLEPT in the upper berth that night. I had always slept in the lower, of course, but Kay had got there first. I remember being a bit annoyed but resigned to the fact that she was a visitor, so that I could not very well ask her to move.

Our ship was rather an old one, and the deluxe cabins had the usual upper and lower berths and a couch under the port. They were considerably larger than the regular cabins, though, and boasted a wicker armchair and a dressing table to make them a bit more fancy. The connecting bathrooms were the most deluxe part about them.

I know when I came on at Sydney my room had seemed very comfortable and pleasant—and I never think of it now without a shudder. The horror of that last ghastly night I spent in it will always be lying somewhere in the back of my mind. I'll never forget it.

I fell into a heavy sleep as soon as my head touched the pillow. I suppose it was dreamless for a while, and then I began to have nightmares. Vague, formless dreams of horror, when I seemed to be lying in the lower berth again. They took shape, finally, when I thought that someone had tied a string around my neck and was pulling it tight. Robert Arnold was standing by, but he merely looked at me coldly and refused to help.

I woke up suddenly, with the cold fear of the nightmare still on me. For an instant I wanted to cry, because I was frightened and because all my drinking had not served to make me sleep the night through.

But I pulled myself together and was just about to turn over and try to get off again when I heard a sound below me. For an instant I lay rigid, clutching the blanket in my hands, then I raised my head sharply and looked over.

Someone was just disappearing out of the door, and I glimpsed the silken sheen of my dressing robe —the one in which I had found Peter's ring. I had told Kay to use it while we were undressing, and, remembering that, I felt a cool surge of relief through all my body. It was only Kay of course.

But where was she going? Had she decided to return to her own cabin? And why—in the middle of the night?

I thought I'd better ask her, so I climbed down hastily and went to the door, but when I looked out into the corridor she had disappeared.

I stood there uncertainly for a moment and was conscious of a rising sense of uneasiness and fear. I was dizzy and faintly sick from the alcohol too. I turned back into the cabin.

I locked the door and told myself that if Kay wanted to come back she could knock. My hands were shaking, and despite the warmth of the night I felt cold. I made my way to the berth and started to climb up, and my foot brushed against a human hand.

I dropped back to the floor with a flooding sense of panic and horror. Kay had gone out—it must have been Kay. Then who—what was this?

I clutched at the chintz curtain that hung on the berth to keep myself from falling and peered in. I could just make out a human form that seemed to be half sitting up. None of it was clear but the eyes —I'll never forget those eyes! They were wide open, and they seemed to stare back at me—cold, blank and opaque.

I tried to scream, and the only sound that came was a queer sobbing moan. I found myself at the door, struggling madly with the lock, but in my wild terror I could not free it.

The next instant there was a dull thud behind me, and I felt that the thing had got out of bed and was coming after me. My back went cold and rigid with the expectation of a hand upon it, and the strength seemed to be ebbing from my slippery desperate fingers as they worked at the lock.

The door gave suddenly, and I was out in the corridor, and then I was at Robert's door without knowing how I got there. It was locked, and I tried to pound on it, but my strength was going rapidly. I could see my own door swinging gently with the roll of the ship, and I expected every instant that some horror would emerge from it and follow me up the corridor.

I was whimpering like an animal, and I began to scratch at the door because I could not pound hard enough to make any noise.

It opened suddenly, and Robert stood there, looking at me coldly. I did not say anything—I couldn't. I stumbled into his room and tried to close the door. My teeth were chattering, and quite suddenly I wanted to laugh.

Through a grey mist I heard Robert saying formally, "If you'll tell me what you want, Miss Bray, perhaps I'll be able to help you."

I laughed then. I laughed—and went out like a light.

CHAPTER FOURTEEN

WHEN I CAME OUT OF IT I was lying on the couch, and Robert was standing at the washbasin. I was dimly and uncomfortably aware that I wore only a thin silk nightgown, but he had put his dressing robe over me as a blanket.

He turned around and came towards me, carrying a glass of water. My mind seemed quite blank, and I just lay there and watched him until a trickle of water down my neck brought me to the realization that my face was dripping wet. That started my brain working, just in time to save myself from the glass of water. I said feebly, "Wait!"

He looked down at me gravely and put the glass aside. "You're better then."

I remembered that he had been annoyed with me, and I said painfully, "What am I doing here in your room when you're mad at me?"

He laughed at that and sat down on the couch by me. "Are you trying to make it up with me?" he asked and, stretching his arm for a towel, wiped some of the water from my face.

I became conscious of voices out in the corridor, and suddenly the whole thing came back to me. I started to shiver, and I couldn't stop.

Robert took my hands and held them firmly. "It's all right now, Carla," he said gently. "You mustn't be frightened."

But I couldn't stop shivering.

"There's one thing," I told him, trying to speak clearly through my chattering teeth. "I am not going to bed again on this trip—I'm going to stay up all the time."

There was a knock on the door, and Robert glanced over his shoulder as the purser stepped in.

Mr. Ogilvie looked very grim. He turned his eyes to me and had opened his mouth to speak when Robert broke in curtly.

"You can't question her tonight. She is in a highly nervous condition, and she doesn't know what she is saying. You'll have to wait until the morning."

Mr. Ogilvie turned on him angrily. "But I must talk to her. She must know something, and every delay makes it more difficult."

"We're on a ship," Robert said coldly. "Nobody can possibly get away. Tomorrow will be quite soon enough—I insist that you leave her alone tonight."

He glanced at me and added, "And will you kindly send a stewardess in here? Miss Bray is going to sleep here for the rest of the night, and I intend to stick around and see that nothing disturbs her. You'd better have a stewardess here in deference to Mrs. Jennings."

The purser backed out, looking angry and defeated, and Robert settled down in the wicker chair, saying something about getting it before the stewardess did.

He looked at me for a while in silence, and I felt childishly grateful to him for not asking me any questions. I felt that I could not talk about it at all.

After a while he stirred and said musingly, "You are by far the biggest nuisance of any girl I ever met."

It seemed enormously funny to me, and I laughed—too long and too shrilly.

"You can laugh," he said, "but I'm going to train you not to be so Victorian. I haven't had a decent night's sleep since I met you. If you don't scream you faint. And mostly you do both."

He spoke carelessly, but his eyes were alert and watchful.

I laughed again, trying desperately to keep my mind off the recent horror.

There was another knock on the door, which was followed by the entrance of Dr. Barton.

He said cheerfully, "Hello, Carla. I'm supposed to look you over and see if you're in a highly nervous condition."

"I'll get even with the old bloodhound for this," Robert said softly.

Dr. Barton grinned at him and then turned to me. I looked at him defiantly.

"I don't know what my condition is," I said and discovered that my teeth, which had quieted down, were chattering again. "But if they try to take me out of here I'll scream and scream. I'm going to stay here till we get to San Francisco." I thought it over for a moment and fielded, "For two cents I'd scream and scream anyhow."

The doctor's face changed, and he turned away abruptly and walked over to the washbasin. He filled a glass, produced something from his pocket like a conjuror and dropped it into the water.

He and Robert approached me together, while I watched the glass warily.

"You drink this down," he said. "I don't want to buy your screams."

I shook my head. "Not if it's going to put me to sleep, I won't. I don't want to dream any more. I'm afraid to. Besides, you might put out the light while I'm asleep, and then I'd wake up in the dark. You may not know it, Doc, but I'm not going to sleep again on this voyage."

That seemed funny to me, too, and I laughed for quite a while about it. Robert and the doctor didn't laugh at all. They talked together for a minute in low voices, and then Robert took the glass and raised me, with an arm about my shoulders.

"Drink it, Carla," he said, "and I'll promise to I leave the light on and sit beside you all the time."

"You won't go away or turn the light out or let them take me out of here?"

"I won't go away or turn the light out—and I won't let them come near you," he said firmly.

I drank the stuff then, and he lowered me to the pillow again, and he and Dr. Barton went off to the other side of the room and did some more talking, and then Dr. Barton went out and shut the door.

I began to get sleepy almost at once.

I saw Robert settle himself in the wicker chair, and through a deepening mist I saw the stewardess come in and perch herself on the straight chair.

I started to laugh again then.

Robert said sharply, "Stop it, Carla! What is it now?"

"You'll still be sitting there when I wake up?"

"Yes."

"And you'll probably have a dagger sticking in you."

I drifted off to sleep to the accompaniment of my own silent laughter.

CHAPTER FIFTEEN

WHEN I WOKE UP it was broad daylight, and after a preliminary yawn and stretch I decided that I was feeling pretty much all right.

There was no one in the cabin with me, and I lay there for a while, thinking over what had happened. Some of the horror was still with me, but in the cheerful sunlight it was faint and unimportant, and my strongest emotion was simple curiosity. I wanted to know what had happened.

A glance at Robert's leather traveling clock showed the time to be twelve noon, and I thought, "Doc's pills must have been knockout."

I put on Robert's dressing robe, which still covered me, and drank a glass of water and decided to go along to my cabin and dress.

I went along the corridor with the robe trailing the floor, but when I got to my cabin I found that the door was locked. I rattled the knob and pushed impatiently' but the door remained closed, and I began to lose my temper. I felt that it was carrying things too far to lock a person out of her room when she had nothing but a nightgown to cover her.

A steward happened along at that moment and stopped when he saw me.

"Your cabin has been changed, Miss Bray."

I frowned at him and said incredulously, "Changed?"

"Yes, miss. If you'll follow me, please."

He lead me to the cabin which was on the other side of Robert's room and opened the door.

I went in and found all my belongings neatly arranged there. My curiosity burned more fiercely, and I began to dress hurriedly. I was dying to know what had happened.

The cabin had a door connecting with Robert's room, which was locked, and a bath on the other side.

I had almost finished dressing when there was a knock on the door and Robert walked in.

He said in a rather aggrieved voice, "So here you are. Of all the hours I spent in that damned chair, you must go and wake up during the miserable half-hour I spent being interviewed by old Ogilvie."

"It doesn't matter, but I'm dying to know what happened. Please tell me."

He looked at me curiously. "You don't know?"

"Nothing," I said earnestly.

He was silent for a moment, and I went on eagerly, "What *was* in the lower berth? I saw Kay leave, but there was something or—or somebody in that bed."

He stared at me and said with obvious astonishment, "You saw Kay leave?"

"Why, yes. At least I thought it was Kay."

"Why?"

"Because of my dressing robe. I'd loaned it to her. I—I saw the dressing robe disappearing out of the room."

"The same negligee that came into my room that time?"

"Yes. But for heaven's sake tell me what happened."

He walked to the window and stared out, his forehead wrinkled in thought.

"That negligee," he murmured. "I can't understand it." He shook his head and turned around abruptly. "Mr. Ogilvie said I was not to question you in any way until he did—or tell you what has happened. So we'll leave it at that."

"Oh, Robert! Tell me!" I cried, almost stamping my foot. "I can't wait any longer!"

"Patience, my little cabbage," he said maddeningly. "Just look around and see if you can find that negligee, and then I'll take you straight up to Scotland Yard, Jr., and you can find out about everything."

He looked unusually sober, though, and I knew that something dreadful had happened.

I looked for the dressing robe, but I could not find it. I turned out everything, and Robert searched with me, but it simply was not there.

We rang for the stewardess who had moved my things, at last. We questioned her, but she declared she had not found the negligee among my things. She remembered having seen me wear it, however, and promised to look about for it.

Robert took me up to see Mr. Ogilvie then.

The purser greeted me almost affably. He told me to be seated and then hinted for Robert to leave, but Robert sat down, too, and took out a cigarette.

Mr. Ogilvie shrugged resignedly and turned to me. He asked me to tell him everything that had happened the night before.

I went over it all wearily and finished up with the missing negligee.

He immediately rang for a steward and gave an order that all stewards were to search for the garment without actually looking through people's belongings. I gathered, though, from the way he spoke, that they were to look through people's things—but discreetly.

He turned back to me and asked me sternly if that was all I knew. I declared it was—and then he told me.

After I had stumbled into Robert's cabin he had rung for the night watchman and had told him to go to my cabin and see what had frightened me.

The night watchman had gone and subsequently had run up quickly and fetched the purser.

They had found Kay lying in the lower berth—dead. She had a piece of thick cord around her neck—the neck had some ugly bruises on it—which had been brought up and slipped through one of the springs on the upper berth, pulled tight and then tied onto the lower berth. This cruel arrangement had raised her to a sitting position, until the knot broke, when she had fallen back to the pillow, with the rope still dangling from the spring on the upper berth.

I remembered the thud that had so terrified me when I was trying to get out of the room, and realized that that must have been when the knot gave.

"You see," said Mr. Ogilvie dryly, "Mrs. Bayliss was considerably under the—er—influence, and that made it all very simple for whoever did it. An easy matter, I judge, to tie the cord around her neck, in her condition, and then pull it tight until she was dead. It was tied to keep continued pressure on the throat and so make certain that she did not revive."

Robert frowned faintly and said, "I very much doubt if it was done that way." But Mr. Ogilvie ignored him.

Poor Kay! I was horrified, and as soon as Mr. Ogilvie released me I went straight down to my cabin and cried as though my heart would break.

CHAPTER SIXTEEN

I GOT UP after a while and washed my face and went on down to lunch. Dr. Barton did not appear, but Chet was there of course—he never missed a meal, no matter what.

He was full of questions, and I tried to answer him as best I could. He declared that he was making investigations of his own and had got almost to the end of the trail when this thing of Kay had put him all out. I tried not to yawn and nodded politely when he went on to say that he had not given up yet but was still working on it and expected to fit Kay in somehow.

I hurried through with my lunch and then went straight up to the boat deck, found a secluded corner and stretched out in somebody's chair. I hoped earnestly that whoever it belonged to had forgotten where he left it.

It was a beautiful day. The sun was warm and bright, and the water was a deep sapphire, with little whitecaps. I relaxed in the chair and gazed out onto the ocean drowsily and began to feel better.

My sense of peace was soon broken, however. I heard voices behind one of the ship's gadgets—I don't know what the things are called, but they spout luxuriantly from the boat deck of every ship. They usually paint them white—and sometimes they get artistic and line them with red. At any rate I heard the voices of Celia Merton and Mr. Imhoff from the other side of the one that concealed me, and I smiled to myself.

We had all thought at the beginning of the voyage that they would be a fine match, and we had all waited hopefully to see the romance bloom, but nothing had happened.

Mr. Imhoff was the type who all his life had had a great fear of entanglements. He was one of those negative sorts of creatures who think that every woman they meet is trying to marry them. So he had kept himself sternly away from Celia excepting when her turn came around. In other words, he treated all the women with determined equality.

As I thought about it I realized suddenly that during the last few days he had departed from this safe-and-sane policy and had been hanging around with Celia pretty consistently. I strained my ears to listen to them with keen anticipation.

Uncle Henry would tell you that eavesdropping is a deplorable habit, but I have found it such a great pleasure that I refuse to give it up. Of course I never sneak around and deliberately put my ears to keyholes, but when a God-given opportunity is handed to me on a golden platter nothing on earth would make me cough or clear my throat. In this instance I kept my ears wide open and closed my eyes so that I could pretend to be asleep in case they discovered me.

Mr. Imhoff seemed to be worried about something and annoyed me by mumbling his words, so that I could not hear all he said, but it went something like this.

"I know . . . but, you see, I might . . . pension, if it came out . . . very strict . . . I thought you . . . it's something that could easily belong to you."

Celia was clearer. "I'll be glad to do it for you, but doesn't anybody know it belongs to you? Because if they don't why would it matter? And if they do, then how could I claim it as mine?"

Mr. Imhoff's mumble took on an edge of impatience. "No, no . . . I've not had a night's sleep . . . you *must* . . . it would be easy for you . . . as an old friend, I ask you . . ."

Celia said, "All right, but I think you're making a mountain out of a molehill."

They moved off then, and I lay trying to puzzle it out. Why should he call himself an old friend of Celia's when he had been attempting to make it quite plain to her that he wished to be nothing more than an acquaintance?

I sighed and took out a cigarette. I decided to try and put the whole thing out of my mind, for I knew that my nerves were pretty well shot by this time, and I felt that there was some hard work ahead of me to try and keep them under control.

I was halfway through the cigarette when my solitude was broken into again. Peter Condit wandered up and lowered himself onto one of the smaller gadgets, with his back resting against the rail.

He smiled at me lazily and said, "I've been looking all over the place for you. I want to talk to you."

"All right," I said wearily. "Go ahead."

He spent a silent moment examining the scupper, and then he raised his head suddenly. "What is Robert Arnold to you?"

"Good heavens! Peter!" I exclaimed in astonishment. "This is not like you."

"Don't misunderstand me," he said quickly. "It's—not what you think. I merely want to know whether I can pick him to pieces in front of you or not."

"Go ahead," I said airily. "I don't mind." But I was suddenly wide awake and alert.

He gave me a curious glance. "Yes. And when I've finished you'll run and tell him everything I've said."

"Oh, rubbish!" I said tartly.

He shrugged and laughed a little. "Well, you know the damned busy-body has got me into a spot of trouble over that ring. He and the Ogilvie fool have just had me up on the mat. It seems they found out I was wearing the thing when I retired, the night of Sally's murder. Arnold said I had intimated that I had lost it a few days before. I told them I hadn't known exactly when I lost it—it was just sometime. If the Arnold man did see it when he saw me for a few moments in the smoke room that night, then I must have lost it on my way downstairs, and somebody must have picked it up. As a matter of fact, I don't believe he did see it on me, as he now admits that he didn't see it on Sally, and if he can tell one lie he could easily tell another. Anyway, they have the damned ring there now, and where they found it, the Lord only knows."

I was thinking that something in his voice and words sounded as though he were very much surprised that they had found it at all.

A shadow fell across my chair, and I looked up to find Robert beside me, with a tray in his hands.

"Tea, miss," he said cheerfully and lowered it carefully to my lap.

I was absurdly pleased. I tried not to sound flustered as I said, "For heaven's sake! How did you know I was here?"

"Sees all, knows all," observed Peter, getting to his feet. "I'll be off," he added and went across the deck to the stairs.

Robert grinned at me. "You know, I don't think he likes me."

"He doesn't," I said, carefully pouring my tea. "He's annoyed about that ring business, for one thing."

He sat on the footrest of my chair and, taking a biscuit from my tray, munched it idly. "They put him through it," he admitted, "but he stuck to his original story—that he had lost it, didn't know when or where— and that's all we could get out of him."

"We?"

He took another biscuit. "Mr. Ogilvie and I are just pals."

"Now tell me," I said slowly, "how did you know that Peter wore his ring all that day at Tahiti? I'm sure I didn't tell you."

"Not directly, but you accused me of lying when I talked about having seen it on Sally, so that I figured you must have remembered Peter wearing it. When we told Peter he had been seen wearing it that day he was a bit confused but insisted that he could not remember when he lost it."

I poured some more tea. "It seemed to me, when he was talking about it just now, that he was surprised it had been found."

He thought this over for a while and then startled me by saying suddenly, "By God, Carla! I think I know why he told Miss Merton to tell you that Sally's body was still in that cabin."

CHAPTER SEVENTEEN

I WAS ALL EXCITEMENT. "Tell me then," I said eagerly. "Why was it?"

But he shook his head negatively. "It's only a wild guess. If it develops into anything I'll let you know."

No amount of coaxing on my part would budge him from this stand, and after a while he went on, saying he had business with the purser. He advised me to stay where I was until it was time to dress for dinner.

I felt depressed and unhappy after he had gone. The approaching night was heavy on my mind, and I had a miserable feeling that I'd never be able to sleep peacefully again. I tried to console myself with the thought that Robert would be close to me, with only a door separating us, but somehow no amount of precaution was sufficient to drive away horror.

I pulled myself together sternly, however, and determined not to let it get the better of me.

I must have slept for a while, for I presently opened my eyes with a start to find Mrs. Jennings perched on the footrest of my chair, busily knitting. I groaned inwardly and quickly closed my eyes again, but it was no use. She had seen me move, and she gave her knitting a shake and prepared to speak.

"It's a lovely day, isn't it?"

"Yes," I said briefly.

Mrs. Jennings always started a conversation with a remark about the weather. It was "Horrid day," "Lovely day," "I could do with just a teeny bit more sun today," or, "If it's going to rain why doesn't it—I can't stand a day that can't make up its mind."

In fact, the weather always seemed most important to her—that and the way people were carrying on. And nobody ever carried on to suit her.

"You poor dear," she said now, "I heard all about the dreadful things that happened to you last night."

"Who told you?" I asked shortly.

But she did not seem to know. She replied vaguely that everybody knew about it.

I closed my eyes again. "I don't feel so well," I said moaningly. "I thought I'd take a rest."

It didn't work of course. She merely said, "That's right—that's just what you ought to do. After all, you haven't had much sleep in the last three days, have you?"

I said, "No."

"And there are others who haven't too." She drew her lips into a thin, straight line, and I could see that she was dying to tell me something.

I longed to snub her, but my curiosity was too strong. I said cordially, "Why, what do you mean, Mrs. Jennings?"

"Well, my dear, I don't exactly envy you the situation of your cabin."

"Why?" I asked wearily. I knew that she would have her little preliminaries.

"I suppose you've noticed that everything has happened either in your cabin or very close to it."

"Yes."

"But you must also have noticed that nothing has happened to him."

I frowned and, without actually moving, somehow withdrew myself from her. Evidently she noticed it, for she finished what she had to say in a hurry— gathering her knitting together and moving away, so that she had to call the last words over her shoulder.

"Why don't you ask him what he was doing in Kay's cabin last night at about one-thirty in the morning?"

So she had fixed the guilt there—and soon she'd be busy spreading it all over the ship. I smiled to myself, shrugged and went off to sleep again.

When Robert woke me up, some time later, the sun was setting and I felt stiff and stupid with sleep.

"I hate to wake you," he said, "but you've only time to dress for dinner, with no cocktails."

I stretched, yawned and murmured, "How can I bear it?"

"Bear it, my eye," he said sharply. "Good thing for you."

I elevated my chin and asked, "Why, please?"

"After what happened last night."

"What do you mean?"

"You know very well what I mean. You said something to me, with intent to insult, which annoyed me enough to leave you to your own devices. Poor Kay—I think if I'd only followed you up and made sure that you locked the door "

I struggled with a sudden ache in my throat. "I know. I'm sorry. I guess I'm almost to blame for the whole thing. I should have locked the door myself." The ache became almost unbearable, and suddenly I was crying.

"Don't cry," he said, "or Mrs. Jennings will think I've jilted you. About Kay—if they had wanted to get her they could have done it easily at any time. She always slept with her door wide open to get the air. Just because it was done in your cabin doesn't mean that it was your fault. Here–take this."

He gave me his handkerchief, and I mopped my face dispiritedly. As I handed it back a sudden paralyzing thought arose in my mind.

" 'If they had wanted to get Kay!' " I gasped. "You mean—you mean, they intended to get me?"

He said evasively, "How should I know? Anyway, you needn't worry about it. From now on there won't be a chance for anyone to get into your cabin at night."

I shivered—and could not stop shivering all the way down to my cabin. It seemed very clear all of a sudden. Someone had tried to get into my room the night after Sally's death—and since I usually slept in the lower berth Kay had been mistaken for me!

CHAPTER EIGHTEEN

AFTER DINNER that night the captain and purser held a sort of court of investigation in the lounge, for the first-class passengers. I heard that there had been one with the second class, one with the third class and several, at different times, with the crew. Now it was our turn.

They put each of us in turn on a sort of witness chair and questioned us, bringing out some surprising things.

Mrs. Jennings was the first to be called. She had an inside minimum cabin, which was right on the main corridor on her deck, and she seemed to have heard plenty. She actually admitted that she slept in the upper berth, where there was a sort of ventilator thing made of narrow shutters, and so had a good view of the corridor.

She explained it away by saying that she suffered greatly from insomnia, and when anyone passed by her cabin, while she was lying awake, she simply could not rest until she had seen who it was.

"Now, Mrs. Jennings," said Mr. Ogilvie, who had been dryly patient through these preliminaries, "I want you to tell me about everyone you saw after you were in bed the night Miss Grable was murdered."

Mrs. Jennings folded her hands, drew in her chin and prepared to enjoy herself.

"I saw Miss Grable go to her cabin, then several stewards passed by, and a stewardess, then Miss Grable came out of her cabin and went to the ladies' room. She came out again—"

The purser cleared his throat. "Er—how do you know she went to the ladies' room?"

"Why, the door is right opposite my cabin—that's why I chose that cabin. Well, she came out of the ladies' room and went back to her cabin."

Mr. Ogilvie interrupted again. "How do you know that she went to her cabin? You could not possibly see her cabin from—er—from where you were."

"She started off in the direction of her cabin," said Mrs. Jennings in an annoyed voice.

"But she might easily have gone across to the other side of the ship?"

Mrs. Jennings gave over and said reluctantly, "Well—yes."

"That would have been at about the time Mrs. Bayliss heard her on her way to visit Mr. Condit."

Peter, who had followed the proceedings with an air of bored indifference, jerked his head up, and the Marsh family started whispering excitedly.

Peter said haughtily, "What do you mean?"

"All in good time, Mr. Condit," said the purser smoothly. "You shall have your chance to speak. And then?" he added, turning to Mrs. Jennings.

"I fell asleep, but I woke up later. I don't know how much later—but I heard Sally pass, and she was with someone. I listened carefully, but I could not identify the other person, so I sat up and looked, but by that time they had gone out of my range."

"You are quite sure it was Miss Grable who passed?"

"Oh yes. She spoke and laughed, but I could not make out what she said. It sounded something like 'past worker.' "

Mr. Ogilvie said, "Hmm," and thought it over for a minute. Then he asked, "Did you hear this other person speak?"

"Once. It was just a low murmur."

"But you don't know whether it was a man or a woman?"

"No. I really couldn't say."

"Did you hear the footsteps of this other person?"

"Yes."

"Were they heavy or light?"

"Well, rather medium."

The purser sighed impatiently. "Were they heavier than Miss Grable's footsteps?"

"Yes."

"Then you could distinguish between them?"

"Oh yes—quite. I knew Sally's step quite well."

"Now, Mrs. Jennings," said the purser, and put all he had into his plea, "I understand that you can't be sure whether this other person was a man or a woman, but what was your impression—you must have had some idea."

"No, I didn't," said Mrs. Jennings sharply. "That's what I was so puzzled about, that's why I raised myself up—tired and all, as I was—to see just which it was."

Mr. Ogilvie resigned himself and said, "Very well, Mrs. Jennings. Now please tell us whom you saw last night."

I felt myself straining forward, my hands twisting in my lap. Now she'd tell about Robert going to Kay's cabin—which I didn't believe anyhow. She pulled her chin in again and said importantly, "I went to sleep early; there was nobody around when I went to sleep, but I woke up at about half-past one and heard someone out in the corridor. I sat up and looked out—and I believe I saw a ghost!" She paused and looked around at us expectantly.

Celia Merton and the Marsh girls gasped appreciatively.

"Explain what you mean, Mrs. Jennings," Mr. Ogilvie said with a touch of severity.

"I looked out just in time to see a grey mist pass by."

"A grey mist?"

"Yes, a grey mist the size of a human form. It just disappeared from my view as I looked out."

"Could you see through this mist?"

"No, I don't think so. But it was so quick, I really don't know."

"Then just why do you describe it as a mist?"

Mrs. Jennings, with an idea that her act was being spoiled, grew cold and annoyed. "I couldn't say," she replied icily.

Mr. Ogilvie delicately mopped his brow and took hold of the bone again. "This grey mist was making footsteps, you say?"

"I did not say," snapped the witness.

"But you said you heard footsteps and looked out to see who it was."

"Yes. But that doesn't follow—"

"Did you see anybody else, at that time, to whom the footsteps could have belonged?"

"No. But that doesn't say there wasn't anyone." She was grimly determined that her grey mist should remain a ghost.

"Well then, did those footsteps sound anything like the footsteps that accompanied Miss Grable?"

Mrs. Jennings considered this for some little time, and at last she said slowly, "Yes, Mr. Ogilvie, they did. They sounded exactly the same."

There was a short silence. I don't know what the others thought, but I was of the opinion that Mrs. Jennings was simply trying for an effect. I couldn't believe that she remembered a positive similarity in two sets of footsteps.

"Then that is all you heard or saw last night?" said Mr. Ogilvie.

She hesitated, drew her chin in for the third time and said firmly, "Yes."

She was excused, and I leaned back and felt myself relaxing. She had not told about Robert going to Kay's cabin—if he ever had.

CHAPTER NINETEEN

CHET WAS EXAMINED NEXT. He did not seem to know anything and said that he always went to sleep as soon as his head touched the pillow. He had not seen or heard anything suspicious at any time; but he managed to intimate to the meeting at large that he was going to track down the person who did it—or else.

After Chet had subsided the Marsh family came on, one by one. Their cabins were near Chet's—at the opposite end of the ship from Mrs. Jennings' dugout.

Sir Alfred replied to the purser's questions in monosyllables, the sum total of it being that he had neither seen nor heard anything strange. Lady Marsh had the same report to give but gave it volubly. Lucy and Phyllis, who shared a cabin, admitted timidly that they knew nothing.

Then Celia Merton was called.

"At what time did you retire on the night Miss Grable was murdered, Miss Merton?" Mr. Ogilvie asked smoothly.

"Around ten o'clock."

"Did you go straight to sleep?"

"No. I was very tired, but I was restless."

"Did you get up again then? Or did you remain in bed?"

She colored, stammered, suffered acutely for a moment and at last gave up the fact that she had got up, some time later, and gone to the ladies' room.

Mrs. Jennings, sitting near me, murmured that the purser was being tactless.

"Did you see anybody in the corridors?"

"Yes," very low and blushing furiously.

Mrs. Jennings clicked her tongue. Mr. Ogilvie looked surprised.

"Who?" he asked eagerly.

Celia said, "Sally," and began to twist her handkerchief in an agonized fashion.

"At what time was this?"

"I don't know. I did not look at my watch when I got up. I just know it was quite some time after I went to bed."

Mr. Ogilvie became stern and forbidding and asked severely, "Why did you not tell us of this meeting before, Miss Merton?"

Celia mangled the handkerchief more desperately than ever. "I did not think it was important," she said faintly and looked as though she expected to be hit for saying it.

Mr. Ogilvie shook his head, clicked his tongue much in the manner of Mrs. Jennings and said in a tense voice, "Continue."

Celia drew a quick breath that was almost a gasp. "She was coming up the main corridor as I came out of the side corridor from my cabin."

"Had she passed the corridor leading to Mr. Imhoff's cabin?"

Mrs. Jennings raised her eyebrows. Celia said, "Er—yes."

"And was she coming towards the corridors leading to your cabin and that of Mr. Condit?"

"Yes."

"How was she dressed?"

She was obviously startled at this question and became confused. There was a long pause before she said reluctantly, "She was fully dressed."

I didn't believe her. It flashed across my mind that she had answered that way to protect Sally's honor.

Mr. Ogilvie evidently had it figured the same way, for he said very gravely, "Miss Merton, we are investigating a murder, and it is *extremely* important to know everything exactly as it occurred. If Miss Grable was not fully dressed, you need not feel that you must protect her. Please tell me exactly what she wore."

Celia sent an anguished glance across the room. I followed her eyes and was astounded to see Mr. Imhoff, sitting somewhat apart from the rest of us, receive it with an expression of the most fearful anxiety upon his face. He was mopping his forehead, which gleamed with beads of perspiration.

I looked back at Celia in time to see her give her head a little toss. She said firmly, "She was fully dressed."

Mr. Ogilvie made an impatient movement, and his face fell into lines of discouragement. I didn't blame him. It seemed fairly obvious that she was lying.

"Very well," he said resignedly. "Did you speak to her?"

"Yes. When I saw her so close to my cabin I remembered a scarf that I had promised to give her. It was a man's scarf belonging to a relation of mine—he had given it to me for a suit I had, but I never wore it much. Sally had said once that she needed a white scarf, so I had promised to give it to her. It had a monogram on it—the letter *I*—in black, but she said she didn't mind that, so when I saw her I gave her the scarf then."

She spoke in a hurried, almost breathless fashion, and when she stopped it somehow left you with the impression that she had broken off in the middle.

"Did you take her to your cabin?" asked Mr. Ogilvie.

"Yes. She came to the door, and when I gave her the scarf she went off."

"Did she thank you?"

"Why, yes," Celia said in a surprised voice. She began to worry her handkerchief again.

"Did she tell you what she was doing in that part of the ship?"

"No."

"Did you ask her?"

"No."

"Will you tell me as much of the conversation as you can remember?"

"It's not much. I asked her about the scarf and she said yes, she'd like it, and when I gave it to her she thanked me and went off."

"In what direction did she go?"

She hesitated over that and then said, "I don't know. I was putting my things straight after having taken the scarf out."

He was silent for a moment and, turning, picked up a briefcase that had been lying on a chair. He unlatched it, and with a sudden movement pulled out my lost dressing robe and held it up in front of Celia's face.

"Ever see this before?"

But Celia looked at the thing indifferently and said, "No."

CHAPTER TWENTY

I WAS a good deal more stirred than Celia appeared to be at the sight of my lost dressing gown. I wondered where they had found it and when they were going to return it to me. I was very fond of it, and it had cost me a pretty penny. I caught Robert's eye and tried to look my question at him, but he just grinned and raised his shoulders slightly.

He was sitting at the table beside Mr. Ogilvie, and I was strongly of the impression that he was putting his oar in by nudging the purser every now and then. I thought idly that Robert would have made a better job of the questioning than Mr. Ogilvie was doing.

Mr. Imhoff was called next. He looked pretty bad—his face pasty and unhealthy pouches under his eyes. Something pathetic in his appearance made me vaguely uncomfortable. In a somewhat misty fashion I connected his agitation with Celia's halting recital of what should have been a perfectly straightforward story. I wanted to think more about it, but I stored it away in my mind and prepared to listen.

"Mr. Imhoff," said the purser, "did you hear Miss Grable pass your cabin on the night she died?"

"No, no," said Mr. Imhoff nervously. "I went straight to sleep that night. I retired at about ten and went straight to sleep. I didn't wake up until seven in the morning."

"And last night?"

Mr. Imhoff was almost apologetic. "The same thing. I retired early and slept all night. It was at breakfast that I first heard about the tragedy."

Mr. Ogilvie tried a few more questions, but the result was negative, and Mr. Imhoff was presently excused. He went off mopping his forehead with a hand that shook visibly.

Peter Condit was called, and there was a buzz of excitement as he walked carelessly to the table. He took his scotch and soda and his cigarette along with him, and he looked half bored, half sulky. He sat down and after one fleeting, faintly hostile glance at Robert appeared to fall into a coma.

The purser said slowly and distinctly, "Mr. Condit, we know that Miss Grable visited you in your cabin on the night she was murdered. Will you give us the details of that visit, please."

Peter raised his eyes, dropped them again and asked with a touch of insolence, "How do you know Miss Grable visited me that night?"

The purser stiffened and said coldly, "We are asking the questions, Mr. Condit. You will do the answering, if you please."

Peter raised his eyebrows, sipped his drink, flicked ash from his cigarette and said at last, "I don't know how you found out about her visit to me, and I'm sure if I denied it you could never prove it on me. As it happens, there's no reason to conceal it, so I'll tell you. She did drop in for a casual visit."

He sipped his drink again, while everyone waited breathlessly for him to go on. Then he drew on his cigarette, emitted a thin spiral of smoke and appeared to lapse back into a state of coma. I could not help admiring his nonchalance.

Mr. Ogilvie waited for a while before he asked with a touch of impatience, "Did she come to see you about anything special?"

"No," said Peter.

"How long did she stay?"

"A few minutes."

"Can't you estimate the number of minutes?"

"No," said Peter.

I began to feel sorry for Mr. Ogilvie. I knew that he had to be more or less polite to these people, and yet some of them had been so exasperating that I would not have blamed him if he had hurled his brief case at their heads.

He let a moment pass and then asked with admirable control, "How was she dressed?"

Peter said quickly, and too glibly, "She was fully dressed."

I felt sure he was lying, and I was sure that Celia had lied. I decided that Celia's evasions had set the course for Peter—and he was never one to pass up an opportunity.

"Did you talk about anything special?" Mr. Ogilvie asked quietly.

"No."

"Then why did you give her your ring at that time?"

There was a minor sensation in the audience, and Peter came out of his coma and flushed darkly.

"I did not give her my ring."

"Did you see her take it?"

Peter made a restless movement and said, "No, but she may have taken it then—I don't know . . ."

"Had you undressed?"

"No."

"Then," said Mr. Ogilvie with heavy sarcasm, "she must have taken the ring on your finger while you were not looking."

Peter crushed out his cigarette, the color still dark in his face. His aplomb dropped away from him, and he became confused.

"I—I don't know what you mean," he stammered.

Mr. Ogilvie dropped the sarcasm and said earnestly, "Mr. Condit, we know that you gave the ring to Miss Grable that night. You were seen wearing it before you retired, and it is known that you never took it off. We have the testimony of your steward for that. You told him that you never removed it, and he noticed that you wore it in bed and in your bath. Therefore we know that you would not have taken it off except for a very special reason. Since that reason was to give it to Miss Grable, we must assume that you were engaged to her."

"No," said Peter sharply. "I was not."

"Then can you explain why you gave your ring to her?"

Peter slumped lower in his chair, stared dejectedly at his drink for a moment and then said heavily, "Oh, all right. I had been somewhat interested in Miss Grable, but she annoyed me from time to time. I did not want to get too much involved—she was too wild. After I had taken Miss Bray out at Tahiti Sally came around that night to reproach me. She became very appealing and asked me for the ring. She said she thought it would keep her straight. I foolishly gave it to her, and then she left. That's really all there was."

"Did you see her along the corridors?"

"I walked to the main corridor with her and let her go on by herself."

"Did you go straight back to your cabin?"

"Yes—straight back, and went to bed."

Mr. Ogilvie turned around sharply and faced Celia. "Miss Merton, did you hear Miss Grable come back past your cabin a short while after she had left you?"

Celia shook her head in a bit of a flutter and said, "No."

"Did you hear her come back at all?"

"No."

"Were you awake for some time after she left you?"

"About an hour," said Celia, and I could see the white flutter of her handkerchief as she began to twist it in her hands.

But Mr. Ogilvie turned back to Peter. "How do you account for that, Mr. Condit?"

Peter spoke slowly and distinctly and with a biting edge to his voice.

"Miss Grable was not with me more than ten minutes at the most—I refused to let her stay—and she might have crossed to the other side of the ship on her return and not passed Miss Merton's cabin."

That was true enough, of course, and Mr. Ogilvie turned away, looking tired and a bit discouraged.

I thought that Peter might have left out the bit about his having refused to let Sally stay. It sounded conceited and mean.

I was startled to hear Lucy suddenly speak up of her own accord.

"Mr. Ogilvie," she said timidly and a little breathlessly, "Phyllis and I have decided to tell you that we believe we saw the grey mist last night."

CHAPTER TWENTY-ONE

FOR A MOMENT there was a startled silence, while we all adjusted ourselves to the idea that Mrs. Jennings' ghost might, after all, have some substance.

Mr. Ogilvie seemed disappointed and depressed, and I suppose that he had evolved some theory which would not support the grey mist.

He asked the Marsh girls about it rather wearily.

Lucy was spokeswoman and was acutely embarrassed over the details of her story. It took a lot of gentle persuasion from both Robert and Mr. Ogilvie, accompanied by a great deal of stammering and a succession of hot blushes on her own part, before the tale was pieced together.

It seemed that when either of them wanted to go out to the ladies' room during the night she always woke the other, and they went together. Last night Phyllis had awakened Lucy, and they had gone out. They had just got into the corridor when Phyllis touched Lucy's arm and gasped, "What's that?" Lucy had looked up in time to see something grey disappear out of the corridor onto the stair landing.

Mr. Ogilvie questioned Phyllis, who said she had caught only a glimpse of it, too, as it disappeared. She was unable to tell from what direction it had come.

That was the extent of their story, and when Mr. Ogilvie asked why they had not told it before they fidgeted uncomfortably and said they had not supposed it was important but had talked it over and finally agreed to tell it anyway.

I decided that the ladies' room angle of their tale had kept them silent at first.

I was called next, and I think I was on the mat longer than anyone else. They took me step by step through all the horror of the last three nights. I was feeling a bit sick by the time I got to the end, but Mr. Ogilvie, without giving me time to recover, proceeded to pull another rabbit from his hat.

"Miss Bray," he said importantly, "why did you tell us that your dressing gown was missing today, when all the time it was stuffed in a corner of your bureau drawer?"

I stared at him, astonished and indignant. "But it wasn't there when I looked for it."

Robert said quickly, "She's right. It wasn't."

The purser turned on him. "Did you look through Miss Bray's bureau drawers yourself?"

"No," said Robert reluctantly. "She did."

"And I repeat," I said firmly, "that it was not there when I searched for it."

Mr. Ogilvie began to look satisfied and happy again.

"Very well, Miss Bray," he said smoothly. "That will be all."

I went slowly back to my chair with a sort of horrified feeling that they were going to put me in irons at any minute. As I sat down with the others my face grew hot with the uncomfortable idea that they might object to having a murderess mingling around with them.

I soon realized that they were not paying much attention to me, because Robert had been put on the stand.

He described the events of the night of Sally's murder and of the following night. Then he said, "Last night I saw Mrs. Bayliss accompany Miss Bray to her stateroom, with the intention of staying with her all night.

"Sometime after I had gone to my cabin I decided to go down to Mrs. Bayliss' cabin to follow out a theory of mine."

Mr. Ogilvie frowned and was heard to click his tongue faintly.

"I went into her cabin," Robert continued imperturbably, "and found nothing to support my theory. But I did find one curious thing."

We all leaned forward in our chairs, and Mr. Ogilvie said alertly, "What curious thing did you find, Mr. Arnold?"

Robert said mildly, "Mrs. Jennings."

"What!"

"I found Mrs. Jennings there."

Mrs. Jennings rose to her feet amid a general buzz of excitement. She said with all the dignity in the world, "That's unkind of you, Mr. Arnold. I did not tell on you."

Robert shook his head at her. "I am under oath, Mrs. Jennings," he said in a voice of gentle reproof.

Mr. Ogilvie's right leg quivered, but he managed not to stamp his foot. "What did you do then, Mr. Arnold?" he asked curtly.

"I thought at first that I had blundered into the wrong cabin, but Mrs. Jennings seemed more confused than indignant, and I came to the conclusion that it was not her cabin at any rate."

"How did you know which cabin belonged to Miss Bayliss?"

"She had taken me down during the day to give me a drink of some special wine she had," Robert said simply.

"Go on."

"Well, I said how do you do to Mrs. Jennings, and she replied rather coldly, 'Not at all, young man.'

"That didn't seem to be getting us anywhere, so I offered her some of the special wine. But matters went from bad to worse, for she merely declared that she was no thief and marched out of the cabin."

He paused for breath and sent a humorous glance into Mrs. Jennings' flushed face.

Mr. Ogilvie said sternly, "Continue."

"I searched the cabin, but I found nothing of any consequence— mostly clothes, no old papers of any sort—nothing, in fact."

"Do you realize that entering and searching a passenger's cabin is a serious offense?"

"I do," said Robert penitently, "but I hope you'll be lenient with me. I was really attempting to solve the murder."

Mr. Ogilvie made an appeal to the passengers at large at this point, and one felt that it came straight from the heart.

"Will everyone kindly leave this investigation to me? It makes everything very much more difficult when several people are investigating at once. I appeal to everyone who has come upon a clue to bring it forward at once."

Nothing happened, of course, and Mr. Ogilvie turned back to Robert, who finished his accounting of the night before and was excused.

Mrs. Jennings was brought back and asked to explain her visit to Kay's cabin.

She was very indignant and said several times that she could not see why it was anybody's business, but Mr. Ogilvie kept at her, quietly and persistently, and she finally backed down.

She said, briefly, that she had been nervous and restless and had got up at last to go to the ladies' room. While she was up she decided to go over and warn Kay to keep her door locked.

She walked off after making this statement and refused to come back, although Mr. Ogilvie called her twice, saying he wanted to ask some more questions.

The meeting broke up then, and Mr. Ogilvie warned us all to lock our doors.

We drifted downstairs, and I realized with a sickish feeling in the pit of the stomach, that another night stared me in the face.

CHAPTER TWENTY-TWO

ROBERT FOLLOWED ME into my cabin as a matter of course and started fooling around with the window.

I watched him for a while and then told him about the conversation I had overheard between Celia and Mr. Imhoff.

"I guess I see it all now," I said slowly. "He was asking her to claim something he had given to Sally—the scarf, of course—and she figured up a way to claim it. Mr. Imhoff is an old fool—and Celia is a fool, too, to do it."

Robert was searching the cabin by this time and had his head under the lower berth.

He said in a muffled voice, "Then Celia probably never saw Sally at all that night. But I think she must at least have heard her, because I don't believe she would smear her conscience to the extent of declaring Sally was there when she did not know whether she was or not." He came out from under the berth and added more clearly, "If you know what I mean."

"No," I agreed thoughtfully, "she didn't see her. That's why she said she was fully dressed—because it would have been dishonorable to say she wasn't dressed when she didn't actually know."

Robert straightened up and dusted off his sleeve with a vigorous hand.

"Well, we'll go into that in the morning. Right now I want to know if you're going to be able to sleep. I've locked up everything in sight, and I can assure you that I've left nothing in here with you that's more than the size of a cockroach. When I go through into my room you can lock the door behind me, to protect yourself from me."

I laughed spiritlessly and said, "I guess I'll sleep all right."

He dropped one of his light, aggravating kisses on my forehead and went through into his room.

I stood where he had left me, feeling lonely and miserable. Not only was I suspected of murder, but I had a nagging fear that someone was trying to murder me. I undressed slowly, making an effort to put it all out of my mind.

It was a trifling thing that finally diverted me. I had promised Phyllis some red nail polish that she had admired and which I never used. I had forgotten to give her the bottle, and of course she had not reminded me. I fell asleep, telling myself that I must take it to her first thing in the morning.

I was faintly surprised when I woke up the next day to find that nothing had happened. I felt refreshed and in better spirits, and I dressed myself with great care. I had not felt so well since that time, only four mornings ago, when I had dressed myself with care for Tahiti and Peter.

I went up on deck and found that it was another beautiful morning. I thought a little wistfully that it might have been a wonderful voyage what with Robert and the weather and everything—had it not been for all the horror.

I shook my head, sighed and went on down to breakfast.

Chet was there, working his way through the usual enormous meal. He looked gloomy and spared me a brief good morning before lapsing into silence again.

I ordered a substantial breakfast and amused myself by speculating on the sort of clothes I'd buy if I got married, sometime or other. I had got to a pair of silver fox scarves when Chet shoved his chair back and got up from the table.

"Excuse me," he said importantly, "but they've got Miss Merton and Mr. Imhoff up before the board, and there's a rumor about that they're practically in irons. I want to go up and see if anybody knows any more."

After he had left I sat for a while feeling uncomfortable and rather mean. I had repeated their conversation to Robert, and of course he had told the purser, and the two of them were in trouble. If I had kept quiet their innocent deception would probably have passed off success-fully—even though Celia was such a poor liar.

I went up on deck after a while. Chet and Dr. Barton were playing a serious game of deck tennis. Sir Alfred was sleeping in the sun, while Lady Marsh, Mrs. Jennings and Lucy and Phyllis were all seated in a group, talking furiously.

For want of something better to do, and feeling faintly curious about what absorbed them so, I went over and joined them.

I sat down on the footrest of Lucy's chair, and I believe Lucy was the only one who noticed me. She immediately started to nudge her mother, but Lady Marsh was not one to take much notice of Lucy's nudges, and she never even faltered. "And he won't do it. I've asked him several times, and he always changes the subject. But of one thing I'm certain—he's married."

"I don't believe it," Phyllis bleated, but Lady Marsh ignored her as usual.

"He behaves like a married man, and if you say there was a woman with three children waving him good-by in Tahiti, then I think that there can be no possible shadow of doubt. He is certainly married. There are a lot of married men who do that, you know. Keep their marriages secret on a voyage, so that they can have a good time with the girls."

She glanced around triumphantly as she finished and, catching sight of me for the first time, gave a little jump.

Mrs. Jennings threw herself into the breach and bravely asked me if I didn't think it was a beautiful day.

I said yes, and then asked them point-blank whom they were talking about.

Lady Marsh looked at me and narrowed her mean little eyes. "Why, as a matter of fact, we were just discussing Mr. Arnold. We believe he is married, because he won't tell anything about his home in Tahiti, and because Mrs. Jennings saw him say good-by to a woman and three children."

"He kissed them all," said Mrs. Jennings firmly.

"How insanitary!" I murmured scornfully. "Did it ever occur to you that it might have been his sister—or some relative?"

"It did," agreed Lady Marsh impressively. "But since he avoids all mention of them and of everything else concerning his private life we have come to the not unnatural conclusion that she must be his wife."

She lay back in her chair and closed her eyes, as though to indicate that the audience was over. Mrs. Jennings busily clicked her knitting needles. Phyllis looked sullen, and Lucy on the verge of tears.

I got up and walked away and thought angrily, "Damn them all!" I decided that I would ask Robert straight out if he were married, and I told myself that I did not believe he was.

I walked over to Chet and Dr. Barton, who had just finished their game and were listening to a steward, who seemed to be giving them a message in a low voice.

Dr. Barton hurried away just before I reached them, and Chet turned to me with a puzzled frown. "It just doesn't fit," he said, shaking his head.

"What doesn't fit what?" I asked curiously.

"Mr. Imhoff," he said. "He's just tried to commit suicide."

CHAPTER TWENTY-THREE

I WAS HORRIFIED. Poor Mr. Imhoff—probably making a mountain out of a molehill, as Celia had said. I felt sure that he was guilty of nothing more than having given or loaned a scarf to Sally.

Morbid curiosity took me down to the purser's office to discover what I could, but there was no activity around the door nor any buzz of conversation inside. I went on to Mr. Imhoff's cabin and heard movement and murmuring from inside. As I stood there a steward came out and walked quickly away. I had just put my ear carefully to the door when it was jerked open, and Robert came out.

He asked abruptly, "What are you doing here?"

"Eavesdropping," I said simply. "Is it true that poor Mr. Imhoff tried to commit suicide?"

He took my arm and led me firmly down the corridor and towards the stairs. "I wish you'd behave yourself," he said mildly. "You're supposed to be relaxing in a quiet corner of the deck—instead of running about trying to find out things."

"I'll go up on deck," I said, "if you'll come, too, and tell me what's happened."

"Oh well—I suppose I must."

We went to the boat deck and dragged a couple of chairs into what might have been either a nook or a cranny—I could not say which—and settled down into them.

Robert stretched his arms above his head, yawned, closed his eyes and said, "Let's go to sleep. Do us more good than a walk."

I cried desperately, "No, no—you've got to tell me all about it. I can't sleep until I know."

He opened his eyes again and sighed. "You are an infernal nuisance, my little begonia. But I suppose you will have it, so listen carefully, don't interrupt and don't ask me to repeat anything."

"Oh, do get on with it," I said impatiently.

"Well, we went into Peter's igloo this morning—early—and woke him up, much to his disgust. He said it wasn't fair, because he never knew what he was saying in the early morning."

"Who do you mean by 'we'?" I asked.

"I told you not to interrupt. I mean Ogilvie and me. He's doing Sherlock Holmes, and I'm his Watson. He can't get rid of me, although he'd give a lot if he could."

I shook my head and murmured, "I don't see how you get away with it."

"Never mind that. We told Peter that we had the testimony of a steward who said he had stood on the landing near the stairs and had seen Sally walk along to Peter's cabin that night. He declared that she had not met Miss Merton and that she was dressed in the nightgown and robe she wore when she was found murdered. He also saw Miss Merton go to the ladies' room, but that was after Sally had disappeared into Peter's cabin. He saw Celia return to her room, and then he was called away. He did not see Sally come out of Peter's cabin.

"We asked Peter, with a small dose of biting sarcasm, if Sally had paid him two visits that night, since he had already testified that she came to see him when she was fully dressed.

"Peter cussed around a bit and then said that there had been only one visit and admitted that Sally had worn her nightgown and dressing robe. He said he had given false testimony because Celia's lies had opened up the way, and he had no wish to make Sally sound any wilder than she had been known to be.

"We knew, of course, that fear and not chivalry had prompted his evasions. He wanted to separate, as far as possible, her visit to him and her murder."

Robert paused and drew a long breath.

"Do they suspect him?" I asked curiously.

"I don't know. Ogilvie is a cagey devil. I tell him all my little theories, but he never tells me his—if he has any."

"You haven't told me any of your little theories," I said resentfully.

"No, darling, but you're such a gossip."

"Why, what do you mean!" I cried hotly. "Here I never tell anybody but you about the things I find—and every time I've told you something it's been all over the ship in ten minutes."

"If you interrupt five more times," he said severely, "I'll go to sleep, and you won't hear about Mr. Imhoff's aspirins."

"His—what?"

"That's once," he said, holding up a finger. "Do you remember me telling you that I thought I knew why Peter had told Celia to make you think the body was still in the cabin that night?"

I nodded eagerly.

"It seemed to me that he had done it to keep you out of the cabin because he wanted to go there himself and search for the ring. I suppose he figured it had probably fallen to the floor, since it was too large for Sally's finger. He was very anxious, of course, to find it before somebody else did. He knew your cabin was next door and knew that you might hear him, but if you thought the body was still there you'd be too frightened to do any investigating. He made a mistake there. He thought you'd figure the intruder to be Mr. Ogilvie or the doctor and let it pass.

But, unpredictable as ever, your first thought was to ring for help."

"Yes," I said slowly. "But was it Peter I heard that night?"

"No. It was somebody else."

"Who?"

"We don't know. It was only by an oversight that the cabin was left unlocked. But we know that Peter, after all his trouble to fix you, actually searched the room before you came down to bed."

"How do you know?"

"We dug up a steward who had seen him in the vicinity around midnight, and when we put it up to Peter he admitted everything handsomely. He insisted that he had made only one visit and after having searched the cabin thoroughly went out and did not come back."

I leaned back in my chair and gave up trying to understand it all. "Give me a cigarette and tell me about Celia and Mr. Imhoff."

He supplied me and lighted up himself.

"We got them both up to Ogilvie's office and sat them down and then asked Celia what she meant by saying that Sally was fully dressed when it was known that she was not.

"Celia went down like a row of ninepins and told us all in a hurry. She had merely heard Sally walk by, and she had felt that it would not be right to say she wasn't dressed when she did not know. She explained that Mr. Imhoff had put his scarf around Sally's shoulders one night when she complained of feeling cold, and Sally had kept it. Mr. Imhoff had felt sure that when they found the thing in her belongings he would be involved up to the neck and might even be accused of the murder. Celia said she had warned him that he was making a fuss about nothing, and now, because of the lies he had persuaded her to tell, they were both in serious trouble.

"The old boy had been sitting quietly through all this, and when Celia stopped speaking we turned to him to ask him what he meant by it. He had a small empty tin box in his hand, and he was chewing vigorously, a slightly wry expression on his face. He held up the box and said, "This used to hold aspirin tablets to relieve my toothache. I have just finished my twelfth.'

"We sent for Dr. Barton then."

CHAPTER TWENTY-FOUR

MR. IMHOFF DID NOT DIE, of course. He was merely indisposed for the rest of the day. We never knew whether he really had intended to commit suicide, or whether he knew, with his vast experience of pills and patent medicines, that the aspirins would not kill him.

The rest of the day was very quiet, but something happened after dinner that made me wonder a little.

Peter asked me to play bridge with him against Sir Alfred and Lady Marsh, who quite fancied themselves as a hot team. I assented reluctantly because I had had vague ideas of walking the deck in the moonlight with Robert.

But he did not seem to be in evidence, so I sat down and we started. The game went along as usual, with Lady Marsh picking apart everything Sir Alfred did, and Peter playing entirely without comment.

Peter and I were winning, and as time went on Lady Marsh became so voluble that I felt I could not stand the sound of her voice for another instant. I was on the point of telling them I must stop when Peter took the bid, and I decided to stroll on the deck and try to recover myself. I was sorry afterward that I had not stayed in my chair—even if it meant throwing my highball at Lady Marsh's head.

I had gone a short way along the deck when I caught sight of a couple locked in each other's arms and engaged in a long, still kiss.

I recognized Robert first, and then as her head fell back a little into the moonlight I saw that the other was Lucy.

I was sure that they had not seen me, and I turned and fled. I stumbled back into the smoke room and resumed my seat with my thoughts whirling. I was no longer conscious of Lady Marsh's piercing voice, and I played several hands in a complete daze, until Peter said tersely, "Let's stop after this rubber."

Lady Marsh did not want to stop, but I insisted, and at about ten o'clock I went down to my cabin.

I locked the doors, fixed the window as I had seen Robert do, undressed and took myself to bed.

I could not sleep, and at every sound I raised my head from the pillow and listened carefully. I realized at last that I was waiting to hear Robert come to his room.

I heard him just as I was dozing off, and he came straight to the connecting door and knocked softly.

I stared at the door balefully, as though it were Robert himself, and then said, as sleepily as I could, "Yes?"

"Are you all right?"

"Of course."

There was a slight pause and then, "Is your window fixed properly?"

"Yes, thank you."

"All your doors locked?"

"Certainly."

Another slight pause. "Well—good night."

"Good night," I said in a dignified voice and immediately turned my face to the pillow and dropped off to sleep.

I slept restlessly and awoke to a grey, misty day that I felt suited my mood exactly.

I was glad that neither Chet nor Dr. Barton was at the table when I went down to breakfast, for I didn't feel like talking to anyone.

After breakfast I got my book and located myself in the drawing room in a deep armchair. I knew that no one but Mrs. Jennings ever went there, and she had often boasted that she never interrupted people when they were reading. She had respect, she said, for other people's occupations and interests.

I tried to interest myself in my book, but my mind kept returning stubbornly to Robert and Lucy. I gave up any attempt to read at last and decided to think the whole thing out and then forget it. But I kept my eyes on the book just as a precaution.

I decided, painfully, that Robert was just the philanderer type and made love to every girl he saw. I was deeply humiliated that I should have been one of a crowd—and I had an uncomfortable conviction that he thought I had taken him seriously. But I was determined that thereafter I would let him see that I was quite indifferent to him. I would be gaily pleasant, but that was all, and he would realize that I had not fallen for him. All very well, of course, except for the one stubborn, nagging little idea that maybe I *had* fallen for him.

My eyes filled, and as I blinked furiously I became conscious of a regular clicking sound that I vaguely realized had been going on for some time. I raised my head and found that Mrs. Jennings was sitting close to me, busily knitting.

She caught my eye and started talking at once. I suppose she figured that if your eyes were not actually on the page it could not be called interrupting.

"I hear that Mr. Imhoff is practically recovered already. Wasn't that a dreadful thing for him to do?"

"Awful," I agreed tentatively, wondering if she'd heard anything new.

"Well," she sighed, "I suppose he must have done the murders. Although I saw the grey ghost again last night."

I stirred uneasily. I did not want to believe in her ghost, but I did not know what to think, since Lucy and Phyllis had backed her up.

"Tell me about it," I said tiredly.

"Well, it was just a glimpse, you know. It was as I came out of the ladies' room; a flutter of grey flew past in the corridor—"

I sat up and stared at her. "You saw it as close as that?"

"Well, no. It wasn't very close. You see, as I turned my head it just disappeared out of the corridor onto the stair landing."

I relaxed again and thought scornfully that it was just like her— upright and honorable and would not tell a lie for the world, but didn't mind arranging a story so that it gave a totally false impression.

"Maybe it was a steward waving a dirty towel," I said indifferently.

She began to gather her knitting together as though she had just been reminded of a pressing duty.

"Well, good-by for the moment," she said with just a touch of acid in her voice. "I must be off. Er —the latest romance seems to be Phyllis and Mr. Arnold. They've been walking the deck together all morning."

She trotted on, and I stared after her with loathing. I felt miserably humiliated. It seemed to me that it must have appeared to everybody on board that I was after Robert, and probably they were all laughing by now. It was hateful to have to accept it, but I made up my mind that it was not going to get me down. I closed my book with a bang and went to my cabin.

I decided to lie down for a bit and, slipping off my dress, I went to the wardrobe for a negligee. As I took it from the hanger I noticed that the dressing robe—the by now famous garment that had disappeared once and that they had returned to me—was gone again. The empty hanger was there, but a hurried search of the wardrobe failed to reveal the thing.

I rang for the stewardess and had her search the cabin, and when she did not find it I told her to go straight to the purser and report it.

CHAPTER TWENTY-FIVE

MR. OGILVIE CAME DOWN in person and carefully searched my cabin. It annoyed me considerably, but I did not quite know what to say about it, so I held my tongue. I knew he was the type who would believe nobody but himself, so I sat in the wicker armchair and watched him coldly while he tossed my underwear about and burrowed around in the wardrobe.

He admitted at last that the thing was gone and looked at me as though he were half inclined to ask me what I had done with it. I raised my chin and eyebrows, and he backed out, murmuring something about an order to the stewards to search for it.

Robert came to the door just as he left.

"Where have you been?" he asked accusingly. "I've been looking for you all morning."

I said, "Oh—good morning," much too brightly.

He looked at me oddly and after considering me for a moment asked, "Well, where have you been?"

"I spent a quiet morning in the drawing room."

His eyebrows went up, and a faint, annoying smile appeared on his face. "Then you must have seen Mrs. Jennings."

"Of course."

"Didn't she tell you I was looking for you?"

I felt a positively animal desire to snarl at this point. I controlled it with difficulty and said, "No, indeed. She told me all about the latest romance, which turned out to be you and Phyllis. She said you were blossoming or something."

He laughed—heartily. "Come on up on deck. We've just time for a brisk walk before lunch."

"I loathe brisk walks," I said coldly. "I'm going to have a cocktail with Peter before lunch."

He stared at me and slowly shook his head. "Someday I shall flirt with Mrs. Jennings, just to see how strong your wicked jealousy is."

I couldn't help laughing a little, nor saying, "You can always have a cocktail with us."

"Thank you," he replied, bowing low. "I'll walk upstairs with you and make up my mind on the way."

We went to the smoke room, and to my utter dismay Peter was not there. I had counted on him, because he always had a cocktail before lunch and always had it in the smoke room.

Robert grinned. "Looks as if Peter had stood you up."

"Don't be silly," I said sharply. "I had no date with him. I simply have a standing invitation to join him when I feel like it."

He continued to grin in a very annoying manner and jerked out a chair for me.

"I shall pinch-hit for the bounder," he said humorously. "I can't let you sit here all alone. What will you have? Steward!"

The steward came running—as they always did when he roared. We gave our order, and I asked about Mr. Imhoff.

Robert said that he had told his story that morning—lying in his berth, with a couple of pillows to prop him up.

Sally, who could not resist flirting with any man who crossed her path, had met him one night on the boat deck, where he had gone for a breath of air. He had worn the scarf for the first time that night to protect his throat, and Sally had danced up to him and pulled it off and put it across her shoulders. She asked him for it then, saying she needed it for a suit she had.

He hemmed and hawed a bit and at last gave in and told her she might keep it. His shock was profound when she laughed and declared that the scarf was a token of their engagement, and she was going to show it to all her girl friends and tell them that she was engaged to the man who had given it to her.

He had spent a dreadful night tossing and turning and the next day had tracked Sally down and asked for the return of his scarf. At first she had pretended that she did not know what he was talking about, but he insisted, and in the end she laughingly told him not to worry, because she had decided to keep their engagement a secret. He had had to be satisfied with that.

"So you can see," Robert finished, looking at me with a humorous twinkle in his eye, "what worrying about trifles brings you to. Practical insanity."

"It seems incredible," I said, "that he should have tried to commit suicide over a small thing like that. And getting Celia into trouble too. It's absurd."

"But there's something more in the thing somewhere," Robert said slowly. "Something . . . but I can't seem to put my finger on it . . . ."

Lady Marsh joined us at that point and ordered a cocktail for herself. She immediately took the floor with her piercing voice, as she always did.

"Do you know," she said, "every morning when I come out of my cabin I find three matches lying on the floor, just over the sill—and always in the same position. I pick them up and throw them out the port, and then there they are the next morning again. They look like the same matches every time too. I'm beginning to get nervous about it."

The luncheon bugle blew just then, and we jumped up like boardinghouse inmates and made for the stairs. Lady Marsh brought up the rear, still talking loudly.

I didn't listen to her or take the trouble to remember about the three matches until it was brought to my attention, later on.

CHAPTER TWENTY-SIX

I FELT A BIT BETTER after lunch. I said to myself several times, "Oh, damn! What if he did kiss Lucy?" Through it all the wife and three children in Tahiti nagged at the back of my mind, and at last I determined to pump him and find out about them, one way or the other. I was very resentful of the fact that he still sat at the captain's table when he could just as well have changed to mine.

Chet asked me to have a game of deck tennis that afternoon, and as he was looking pretty mournful, I agreed. We had a long hard game— Chet never played any other way—and when it was finished he asked if I would have tea with him in a secluded spot where no one would find us, as he wanted to talk to me.

I agreed at once. I hoped that he would kiss me and that Robert would see it accidentally. I resolved that if the opportunity arose I would make the kiss a good one—and I even went so far as to go down to my cabin and primp a bit.

I might have saved myself the trouble. Chet barely spared me more than a glance or two, and when he did look at me it was with vague, troubled eyes that never saw me. He was gazing out at the sea most of the time.

He had found a place on the boat deck, near the railing and more or less surrounded by gadgets, and after seating me there he went off and got the tea.

He did not say much at first—he was too busy eating—but when he had finished he clasped his hands on his knee and plunged into it. He was sober and downcast and seemed almost to have persuaded himself that he had actually been engaged to Sally.

He said slowly, "My investigations have led me to someone, but I am sure I'll never be able to get any proof. He's too clever—he's vilely clever."

"Who is it?" I asked patiently.

"Oh, you wouldn't believe me. There's no use telling you . . . but I want to warn you. When you go to bed at night don't let anyone—any-one, mind you—in with you."

"I don't," I said shortly.

He colored and said in some distress, "Oh, I don't mean—mean— you know—casually. But you mustn't let anyone in—not even those you trust—not even me."

I wanted to smile, but he was too much in earnest. "I'll be very care-ful," I assured him, and my jaw grew rigid as I suppressed a yawn. I was getting bored.

He nodded as though satisfied, and then, dropping his eyes, he said almost painfully, "There's—something else I wanted to tell you. I—well, I've got to tell someone. It's—it's getting me down. As a matter of fact, I—hear Sally crying, almost every night."

The sense of horror, that had quieted down, seemed to uncurl again in me. I gripped the arms of my chair and sat up straight.

"What are you saying, Chet?"

"It's true," he said doggedly. "I thought I was imagining things at first—going balmy, you know—but I didn't imagine last night.

"I heard her first the night she was murdered. She was just crying softly, and I didn't know who or what it was. I looked out into the corridor, but there was nobody there, and it had stopped by then anyhow. The next night I heard it again, so I ran out quickly and looked around, but there was absolutely nothing there. It was so familiar all the time— the sound of it—and then I realized that it was Sally's voice."

"Did you ever hear her cry?" I asked.

"Yes, once; and this is exactly like it. The night Kay was murdered I didn't hear anything. Then last night I heard it again. It's so close, almost as though it were in the cabin, and it's Sally's voice! I swear it is!"

"Chet!" I said sternly. "It's not Sally's voice. You've got to get that out of your head. It's somebody else—a stewardess or someone who has something on her mind. Women sound so much alike when they cry."

Chet jerked himself to his feet, his face stony. "I knew you wouldn't understand," he said and stalked off.

I felt a little hurt about it. I thought I did understand, and, after all, I had only tried to help Chet over one of the hurdles that confront all of us from time to time.

My mind drifted back to my own troubles, and I wondered what I ought to do about it. I decided at last to put on my best dress and my coolest manner.

I was glad I had dressed up, later, for when I walked into the smoke room before dinner I found the Marsh girls dolled out in what must have been no less than their ball gowns. When they saw me they explained eagerly that the captain had decided on another dance to cheer everybody up.

I closed my eyes for a moment and shivered. Sally and Kay had been so much a part of the dances that it seemed like making a festival of their funerals. And there were so few of us!

But Lucy and Phyllis were excited and smiling and full of eager anticipation. The captain's methods seemed to work with them at any rate. The dance had taken their minds off all the horror.

We sat down in our finery and ordered cocktails. Peter joined us after a moment, and then Robert, and finally Dr. Barton. We talked and laughed a great deal, and several times I caught Robert's eye, and he half winked at me.

I began to feel happy and to enjoy myself. I was forgetting about Robert kissing Lucy and about the wife and three children in Tahiti when suddenly everything changed to unpleasantness.

It was Phyllis who did it. She and Lucy had been talking a lot and were getting more thrilled and pleased with themselves every minute. I guess they thought they were taking Sally's and Kay's places, and they felt successful or something—anyway, they kept making silly remarks which fell pitifully short of Sally's wit and Kay's sophistication.

Dr. Barton said something about "us bachelors", and Phyllis giggled and cried out, "But I don't think Mr. Arnold is a bachelor, because Carla told us she saw him kiss his wife and three children good-by at Tahiti—and one of the children called him 'Daddy.' "

"Why, Phyllis!" I gasped and was about to deny it when Robert cut me short. One look at his face was enough to show me that he was in a cold fury.

"The trouble with Carla," he said evenly, "is that she wants all the attention for herself alone and doesn't care what she does to get it. Come on, Lucy, what about a walk before dinner?"

Lucy went off with him, her eyes sparkling and her thin face flushed and animated, and I was left sitting there like a fool, conscious of the fact that Peter was regarding me with a faint, lazy smile. I was so confused that I never asked Phyllis what the devil she meant by it.

She looked distressed and said timidly, "He—he seemed to be angry, didn't he? I hope I didn't—I mean—I didn't know he'd be so angry—"

"You shouldn't tell lies, Phyllis," I said quietly.

She seemed on the verge of tears and stammered, "But I'm sure—"

"Oh, hush!" I said impatiently. "Don't worry about it. It doesn't matter. I'm going down to dinner—my head aches."

We went down to dinner then, and all through that wretched meal I kept telling myself that I must stop worrying about things, and the sooner the better. My headache was getting worse.

When the meal was over at last I felt that I would have to get an aspirin, and I started towards my stateroom. I did not want to go, for I hated spending any more time there than was absolutely necessary, but the throbbing in my head urged me on.

My corridor was deserted and seemed dimly lighted and shadowy. I was still some distance away from my door when I saw a misty, undulating grey form come out of my room and disappear from the corridor towards the other side of the ship.

CHAPTER TWENTY-SEVEN

AFTERWARDS I knew I should have hurried after the thing and tried to find out what it was, but at the time I simply couldn't. I stood there all alone, with no sound but the creaking of the ship, and began to shake all over. As soon as I could move I turned and fled to the purser's office.

Mr. Ogilvie frowned, clicked his tongue a bit, but came along immediately to investigate. I followed him timidly.

When we got to the spot where I had been when I saw the thing he asked me to go to my room and then come out so that he could get an idea about it. I refused, though, point-blank. "It might be back in there," I said and tried hard to keep my voice from shaking.

He shrugged impatiently and after marking the spot where he was standing walked with me to my room and made a hasty search. There was no one there, of course, and it did not look as though anything had been disturbed. He went out again, walked back to his spot, and when he was ready I slipped out and across the corridor as I had seen the thing go.

Mr. Ogilvie walked back again. "It's a great pity this light was not on," he said irritably, indicating a dark bulb near my door. "Anyway, tell me all you can remember about it."

"There's nothing much to tell," I said slowly. "It was grey and—and somehow fluttering, and it seemed to float across the corridor in an instant. That's really all I can remember about it."

Robert came along just then, and Mr. Ogilvie stopped him and explained what had happened while I studied my right thumbnail very carefully. Robert, without looking at me at all, coolly told the purser not to pay too much attention to it, since the passengers were generally in a highly nervous state and were bound to make ominous the most ordinary things.

Mr. Ogilvie looked surprised and a bit puzzled as Robert brushed past with a little hunch of his shoulders and disappeared into his cabin.

I turned indignantly to the purser, but he murmured something about his duties and went off.

I went into my cabin, banged the door and sat on my berth for five minutes, enjoying a fit of pure temper. It passed away after that, though, and I felt flat and low spirited.

I got up and took two aspirins and then went to the dressing table and carefully fixed my face.

I decided to go upstairs and have as much fun as I could with Peter. He was always easy with me—witty and good company—and most certainly never, at any time, would he seek the company of the Marsh girls and leave me sitting to amuse myself as best I could.

I was just closing my door on my way out when some curious sense of disarrangement caused me to look in again. I stood there for a while, puzzled and trying to bring to consciousness something that had been at the back of my mind all the time. And then I saw it. My crystal bottle of smelling salts, of course. I never used it, and the bottle had stood on one of the little shelves above the dressing table. I had never moved it, and I doubt if the steward had bothered even to dust under it. It stood, now, right in the middle of the dressing table and forced me to the conclusion that somebody had been in my room. On an inspiration I rang for the steward, and after he had assured me that he had not touched the bottle I sent him to fetch the purser.

Mr. Ogilvie looked very dour indeed when he came, but I soon cheered him up.

I explained about the bottle. "Now if you can only get the finger-prints on it you can at least clear up the grey mist business and shut Mrs. Jennings up for a while."

He refused to smile, but there was an eager glint in his eye. He picked the bottle up with a handkerchief and carefully wrapped it. He stood for a moment looking at it, and I could see the eagerness and enthusiasm slowly fade from his face. "It's no use," he said bitterly. "I have no fingerprint apparatus and would not know how to use it if I had."

"But don't you just drop a little powder on it or something?" I asked desperately.

He thought for a moment and then raised his head suddenly. "Is Mr. Arnold still in his room?"

"I don't know," I said coldly.

He put down the bottle and went out into the corridor, and I heard him knock on Robert's door. There was a murmur of voices, and the next minute they came back together.

Robert nodded distantly to me as he came in. I made no answering sign beyond a slight elevation of the eyebrows.

Mr. Ogilvie was almost excited. "Mr. Arnold says he thinks he might make a stab at it."

I glanced carelessly at Mr. Arnold and said indifferently, "Oh well, I guess I'll leave you to it."

I left them and went up on deck. They were putting up colored lights and otherwise preparing for the dance, so I went into the smoke room.

Celia Merton was sitting with Peter and was awkwardly smoking a cigarette. I joined them and accepted Peter's offer of a drink. I made up my mind not to play with anyone but Peter until the end of the ghastly voyage.

Lucy and Phyllis, complete with ball gowns, were sipping creme de menthe, and Lucy was smoking a cigarette and trying to keep the smoke out of her eyes. Phyllis couldn't smoke. I'd seen her try often enough, but it always ended in a fit of coughing and running eyes, and appar-ently she'd given up the effort.

Chet was sitting by himself in gloomy silence, and Sir Alfred, also alone, except for a whisky and soda, looked as though he could not make up his mind whether to go to sleep or not.

We heard the dance music start up after a while, and Lucy and Phyllis rose as one woman and rustled out onto the deck. Celia half started up from her chair but, observing that Peter and I made no move, she sank back again and lighted another cigarette.

Lady Marsh came in presently after calling a shrill good-by to Mrs. Jennings at the door. I figured that they had been gossiping in the drawing room.

She looked around vaguely for the girls and then walked over to Chet.

"Aren't you going to dance?" she asked brightly.

Chet came out of his abstraction and blinked at her. "Eh? Oh—yes. I suppose so." He got up and wandered out.

Her eye fell on us next, and she came over and repeated her question.

"We can't go yet," I said flippantly. "It isn't fashionable to attend a dance in its early stages."

She took me quite seriously. "Well, but, come now —you don't have to be so formal when there are so few of us on board."

Peter stared at her coldly and said, "When you get Sir Alfred out then we'll come too."

"But you know he doesn't like the dances." She gave it the long *A*.

Peter stirred restlessly and murmured, "Then neither do we."

But the woman actually went over and dragged her reluctant husband out to the festival, and there was nothing left for us to do but follow.

Robert was there, pushing one of the Marsh girls around, and Chet had the other.

Peter said, "Let's dance and satisfy the blasted woman."

Dr. Barton asked Celia, who hopped off under his expert guidance, looking very pleased with herself.

I danced mostly with Peter. He did not dance with anyone else, but I knew that it wasn't because he had any special fondness for me. It was merely that, to his way of thinking, there was no one else to dance with. He would not have dreamed of dancing with Celia, who would have been out of step half the time, and I know that, over and above the fact that he did not like them anyway, he felt that the Marsh girls and Lady Marsh were not sophisticated enough for him.

I danced once or twice with Chet and more often with Dr. Barton, but Robert never asked me once and never spoke to me.

I tried not to care or to think about it, but the dance was a pretty dreary affair for me, and when Peter finally went to bed with a headache I left the thing and went off to a dark part of the deck, where I stretched out in a deck chair.

After a while and because there was nothing else to do I drifted off to sleep.

CHAPTER TWENTY-EIGHT

I WOKE UP to the feel of rain on my face and after a preliminary stirring discovered that I was chilly and stiff. I could not hear anything but the faint throbbing of the engines and the swish of water, and I began to wonder how late it was.

I thought of Robert and wondered if he was still dancing with the Marsh girls, but a moment later I realized that the music had stopped and the dance was probably over. I decided to go and get a drink; I'd join any party that would have me.

I turned my head to look at the smoke-room windows—and stiffened in my chair. The smoke room was dark!

It was late then. Much later than I had thought. Everybody must have gone to bed, and no one had noticed me sleeping in my chair. Or perhaps someone had noticed—perhaps the person who had murdered Sally and Kay had seen me—and was waiting.

I shuddered and cowered in the chair, afraid to move. I looked down the dark expanse of the deck and saw that there was just one small light at the doorway that gave on to the stairs. There were still shadows all around it, and though I strained my eyes fearfully I could see no movement.

I gathered my courage together and forced myself out of the chair. I wanted desperately the haven of my cabin and was horribly afraid of the empty stairs and corridors that led to it.

I started towards the inadequate little light and I had not gone more than a few steps before I stopped dead, sure I had seen something move. I stood there sweating and trembling, but the shadows were still, and there was no sound, and at last I began to move forward again. I gained the doorway and slipped through, but it was even worse inside. Dark entrances to great, empty lounges seemed to close in around me, and the stairway yawned in front of me, dimly lighted and promising some horror in the darkness below.

I tried to set my chattering teeth and forced myself to go down, one clammy hand sliding and clutching at the bannister.

I reached my deck at last and started down the dim, empty corridor. I wondered wildly where the night watchman was and wanted to call out for him, but I was afraid, somehow, of my own voice. My legs were trembling, and I was shivering.

I was halfway down the corridor and nearing my door when a sound of some sort fell distinctly on my ears, and I stopped again. I stretched out a hand to the wall to steady myself and stared at my closed door with dilated eyes.

As I watched, my breath coming in shallow gasps and my heart pounding, I saw the knob turn and the door swing slowly inwards.

I felt my body sag against the wall, and I realized with sharp, wild terror that my legs were giving way and that my voice was gone. My eyes, fixed and staring, remained on the doorway.

For an instant of breathless, mounting horror nothing happened— and then a misty, fluttering grey form stepped out into the corridor and started towards me.

Sheer insane panic gave my legs renewed strength, and with a scream that was nothing more than a moan in my throat I turned and fled. I ran with incredible speed, whimpering like an animal and with no idea of destination. I had only a blurred, desperate desire for sanctuary of some sort.

I turned at last into a side corridor that led to four empty cabins. I fumbled at the doors and found each one in turn locked. I backed down the corridor and cowered against the built-in chest under the porthole.

My temporary burst of strength had gone, and my body slid helplessly to the floor as the ghastly grey image turned into the corridor and bore down on me.

I felt my senses leaving me and can only dimly remember raising my dull, failing eyes to where its face should have been—only there was no face. There seemed to be a few undulating, curving grey lines, and that was all.

My head fell forward, and as the thing closed in on me I slid into blackness and silence.

CHAPTER TWENTY-NINE

THE NEXT SENSATION that cane to me was that of being carried by someone, although for a while I was still walled in by blackness. Then I opened my eyes and saw Robert's face, and I realized vaguely that he was carrying me along a corridor. I felt dimly safe and pressed my face gratefully against his shoulder.

Things faded a little, then, until I found myself lying in my bed while Robert stood at the door, talking in a low voice to a steward. My head ached violently, and my throat felt stiff and sore.

As Robert finished talking to him the steward glanced over at me, and I saw his eyes open wide, with a startled expression. The next instant he had disappeared, closing the door gently behind him.

I stirred and said faintly, "What happened?"

Robert looked around sharply and then came over to me. "'That's what I'd like to know," he said gravely.

I frowned, trying to concentrate and trying to keep any thoughts from sliding away into the darkness again. After some moments of mental confusion I sighed and said, "Will you please hand me a mirror?"

I could see that he thought my mind was wandering, and I explained fretfully, "The steward, you know. He was shocked when he looked at me, and I want to see—"

"No," Robert said definitely. "You would not like it, and anyway, it's only temporary. If you're feeling strong enough will you tell me why you left your room in the middle of the night?"

"But I didn't," I cried, moving my head from side to side. "I didn't. If I could only have got to my room I'd never have come out again. Never."

He said slowly, "But I don't understand. I heard you go into your room at about one o'clock. Then I woke up, to hear you leave again, about half an hour ago."

I stifled a desire to laugh because I had an uneasy feeling that if I once started laughing I'd never stop. "You're a rotten sleuth," I said. "I never came into my room, so of course I didn't go out either. What you heard was that grey thing—that dreadful grey creature that hasn't any face. Did you know that it hasn't any face? But it can run. You can't get away from it. I couldn't—I tried all the doors, and they were locked—"

I began to shiver violently, and Robert said sharply, "Stop it! You're not to think about it."

Think about it! As though I could do anything else. I continued to shiver, and I didn't want to laugh any more. I wanted to cry and perhaps to scream.

Dr. Barton came in just then and after looking at me began to mix one of his concoctions. I decided that it was one of those things that make you sleep, and I took it eagerly, and, more than anything in the world, I wanted to reach San Francisco. Only San Francisco was still four days away, and those four days had to be lived through somehow.

I drowsed off to the sound of Dr. Barton telling Robert that I would not be able to stand much more of this, that he would not answer for me if anything of the sort happened again. I agreed with him thoroughly and wanted to tell him so, but I was too sleepy.

I woke up early. I knew it was early because I could see the sun through the window. Robert was sitting in the wicker armchair with his head thrown back—fast asleep.

I crawled out of bed and made my way unsteadily to the bathroom. My legs were wobbly and felt very unsafe, but I managed to wash up a bit, and on my way back to bed I paused by the dressing table and looked in the mirror.

It gave me quite a shock. My neck was red and badly swollen, and my eyes were bulging oddly. I had never been guilty of popeyes!

I uttered an exclamation, and Robert came awake with a jerk and said, "What's the matter?"

I slipped back into bed. "Nothing. I just looked at myself in the mirror. What did happen to me last night?"

"What did you do?" he countered. "Where did you go? Tell me that, and then I'll tell you how I found you."

I told him everything, and he listened with deep attention.

When I had finished he said slowly, "Then it was somebody else that I heard. You see, I had been waiting " He stopped abruptly.

I laughed—unpleasantly. "Go on," I said derisively. "I won't misunderstand your waiting up to hear me get in safely. I quite understand it was because you felt obliged to look after me, since I am a woman and alone, but for you, in this section of the ship."

He froze up noticeably but continued his story. "I heard someone come in and thought it was you. Whoever it was moved about a bit and then became quiet. That was at about one o'clock. I went to sleep, and some time later the person woke me up by trying the door into my room."

I raised my eyebrows at that and wondered if he had gone to the length of locking his door because he was annoyed with me.

He must have known what I was thinking, for he went on rather brusquely. "As you know, the door is unlocked on my side and locked on yours. Naturally I thought it odd that you should push on it when you knew you had only to unlock it if you wanted to come in. Evidently the person, whoever it was, did not know that and simply tried the door for some reason. I heard the other door open and shut after that, and steps in the corridor, walking away. I couldn't understand why you should walk off like that in the middle of the night, so I decided to investigate."

"Along about that time," I said airily, "you made up your mind that I was the murderer."

He ignored that and went on coldly: "By the time I had found my bathrobe and slippers and got to the door there was no one in sight. I walked around a bit and finally went over to the other side of the ship. I was considering knocking up Ogilvie when I heard footsteps over where I later found you. I went in that direction, but I had to cross the ship, so I must just have missed the person who tried to kill you."

I shuddered and faced for the first time what I had really known since Kay's death: Someone was trying to kill me! I thought wildly that I'd probably be dead, like the other two, by the time we got to the Golden Gate.

I fingered my swollen neck and whispered fearfully, "Was there—was there a cord around my neck ?"

"Yes. The other end of it had been tied to the porthole above you, but not very securely, so that it had slipped off. I don't know whether the pressure on your neck was enough to have strangled you, as it was, or not."

I took a deep breath and said, "Well, thanks for saving my life."

He brushed it aside impatiently, and I closed my eyes rather wearily. I felt sick and faint.

Before I went to sleep again I heard him murmur thoughtfully, "The same kind of cord that was used on Kay—it comes from the barbershop, and the steward says he has not sold any of it."

CHAPTER THIRTY

I WOKE UP to a light tapping on the door, which was followed by the entrance of a stewardess bearing a loaded tray. The sun was shining, and a glance at the clock showed that it was half-past ten.

The stewardess arranged the tray on my lap and said, "I hope you'll like this, miss. Mr. Arnold told me to bring it all. He said you'd probably find something you like on it—but I always say it's better to let a person choose for themselves—only he said you'd just refuse to have anything. He said I was to tempt you with all these things but like as not the sight of them will make you bilious."

I looked at the tray and burst out laughing. It was simply crammed with appetizing little bits of infinite variety.

The stewardess went out, shaking her head, and I proceeded to eat what I could. It wasn't much, though, for I still felt far from well, but the thought that Robert had seen to my breakfast pleased me. He had sat up with me all night too. I thought dryly that I was at least keeping up with Lucy.

Dr. Barton came in after I had finished eating and told me to get dressed when I felt like it and go up on deck.

He breezed out, and on his heels came Mr. Ogilvie, looking very grim. He questioned me at length and in detail for over half an hour, and when he had left I took an aspirin and got dressed.

I went up to the boat deck and sat myself down in a prominent spot. I felt sure that someone would be along presently and at least I would be the center of attention for a while.

But I sat there all the morning, almost unnoticed. Chet came along once and sat beside me for a while. He did not say much beyond the fact that he wished like hell the voyage was over—he was fed up with the whole business. I gathered that he had entirely given up his sleuthing activities.

Mrs. Jennings appeared after Chet had gone away and tossed me a bright "Good morning." She added that it was a lovely day, wasn't it, and passed on.

Celia Merton, busy taking her morning walk, said, "You don't look very well this morning."

The Marsh girls walked by, and Phyllis tripped over something and went sprawling onto the deck. She got up, very red in the face, and murmured something about having turned her ankle. Lucy gave me a fleeting smile.

It suddenly occurred to me that not one of them had mentioned my experience of last night. Either they had been told not to mention it because of my health, or else it was being kept a secret.

The luncheon bugle went, and I started down, determined to find out why I had not been mobbed with questions.

I managed to ask Dr. Barton about it, sotto voce, while Chet was busy shoveling food into his mouth.

"Good Lord!" said the doctor in an agitated undertone. "I was supposed to tell you—and forgot. They're keeping it a secret, or trying to."

Chet came up from the food trough and eyed us inquiringly. "What is it?"

"I was just telling Carla about the flying fish," Dr. Barton said smoothly. "We've known them to fly right through a port into the dining saloon."

Chet said, "I've heard that tale, but I never really believed it."

The doctor raised his eyebrows and murmured, "Really?" but Chet had gone back to his food.

I went back to the boat deck after lunch. I was feeling ill again, and I stretched out in the sun and presently went to sleep.

At four o'clock a steward brought me a special tea. Chet wandered up while I was eating it and gave it a few longing glances. Phyllis appeared shortly afterwards with a box of chocolates, which she offered around. Chet ate nearly the whole box, and then Phyllis suggested some deck tennis, which took them off.

I went down to my cabin at six o'clock to take a bath and dress for dinner. I hated to go into the place, but I set my teeth, flung open the door and made a hasty search. No one was there, so I locked the door and proceeded to get into my bath.

While I was splashing around I heard Robert go into his room, and he came straight to the connecting door and knocked. It was a very inconvenient moment, really.

I called out, "What is it?"

"Is everything all right?"

"Certainly."

"Is your door locked?"

"Of course," I said impatiently. I wondered whether he thought he was noble to take so much trouble over my safety when he was mad at me.

He did not say anything more, and I heard him moving about, getting dressed.

I dressed in a hurry and went straight upstairs. I had come to hate the sight of my cabin, and I wanted the company and cheerfulness of the smoke room.

When I got to the door the first person I noticed was Mr. Imhoff. He was sitting by himself, doing nothing, and he looked dreadful. The skin on his face was hanging in loose folds, and he seemed to have lost pounds.

Peter, Chet and Lady Marsh were sitting at another table, and at the moment they were laughing heartily. I felt sure, somehow, that they were laughing at poor old Mr. Imhoff, and it annoyed me so much that I went over and joined him.

He looked at me and edged away a little as though he were afraid of me.

I said as brightly as I could, "How are you feeling tonight, Mr. Imhoff?"

He merely made some sort of grunt, and I tried again.

"Only three more days, and this dreadful voyage will be over." I spoke with genuine feeling, but I wondered if it were quite the right thing to say.

To my surprise he came to life and spoke eagerly. "Yes, yes—only three more days. It's been terrible for all of us."

"Indeed it has," I agreed and wondered what on earth I could say next.

I glanced around idly and then studied a chair carefully as I saw that Robert was standing in the doorway. He took a quick look around and made a step towards Celia and the Marsh girls, who were sitting looking at three cocktails which they did not seem to be drinking. Then to my surprise he changed his course and came over to us. I felt that he must have decided to hoist the white flag.

Robert called for the steward, sat down and said impersonally, "What will you have, Carla?"

"Sherry," I said nonchalantly.

"Mr. Imhoff?"

"Oh, no—nothing. I could not touch anything in my condition." He slipped a pill into his mouth and began to chew nervously. I wanted to laugh and covered it up by diving for a cigarette. Robert leaned towards me with a lighted match and an absent look in his eyes.

I thanked him coldly and waited for him to say something nice and interesting to me.

He said something nice and interesting to Mr. Imhoff instead. He talked of the relative merits of the school system in Australia and the United States. Mr. Imhoff came out of his shell and was quite like his old self for a while. He began to argue with a certain amount of heat, and Robert kept him going deftly. I began to be pretty sure after a while that Robert hadn't any idea of what he was talking about, and I wondered why he was doing it. I got bored first and then angry. I finished my sherry, stood up and asked to be excused. Robert rose absent-mindedly and nodded coolly to me. I don't know what Mr. Imhoff did.

I went straight over to Peter and said, "Scotch," without any further explanation.

Peter smiled and ordered it for me. "Leading lady returns to first love," he murmured.

CHAPTER THIRTY-ONE

I PLAYED BRIDGE again that night. I wasn't really feeling well enough, but I hated to go down to my beastly cabin and lie there trying to sleep.

I played with Peter against Sir Alfred and Lady Marsh, and we had not been at it long when the smoke room was completely deserted except for our table.

Once when I was dummy hand I strolled to a window and looked out onto the deck. Someone was lying in a deck chair nearby, and on closer inspection I recognized Celia. She had a handkerchief up to her face, and I came to the conclusion that either she was crying or she had a toothache. I was just going out to see if I could do anything for her when Chet sidled up to me and spoke in a low voice.

"Damn it," he said miserably, "that crying is going on again, and I can't sleep."

"Where does it come from?" I asked curiously.

"I don't know." He rumpled his hair fretfully. "It sounds as though it were in the corridor, but when I go out there to look for it, it stops. I went out twice, and both times it stopped. After the second time I went back to my cabin and got dressed. I couldn't stand it any more."

"Did it start again when you were dressing?"

"No," he said dully, "but I knew it would if I got back to bed again."

I considered it for a moment and then said seriously, "You'd better go and tell Mr. Ogilvie about it. I think he ought to know."

But Chet shook his head rather hopelessly. "No, it's no use. He couldn't do anything. It's Sally—I know it is. He wouldn't even hear it because it's meant for me. I'll just have to face it—I'll have to go down again and listen to it."

I was called back to the table then, and Chet squared his shoulders as though he were going to do battle and went off. I watched him and saw that he did not go downstairs again but went out on the deck.

I noticed, too, on my way back to my seat, that Lucy and Robert were sitting together on a small settee in the hallway. I wondered why they had chosen such an uncomfortable spot—and tried not to wonder why they were sitting together at all.

My next dummy hand was not for some time, and when it came I went back to the window to see if Celia was still there. I thought I'd ask her if there was anything I could do for her, but when I looked out I saw that she had gone.

The game went on until twelve o'clock, when Sir Alfred announced that it was his bedtime. It seemed to me it should have been his bedtime long ago, for he and his wife wrangled endlessly, and it was both embarrassing and annoying.

Peter and I collected from them, and we went out.

To my surprise Robert was still sitting in the hall—but alone. Lucy had gone. He stood up as we came out and followed us down without a word. We said our separate good nights to the others and continued up our corridor in silence. When we were almost at my door Robert spoke—rather sharply. "I don't know what Barton thinks he's doing, letting you stay up so late after your experience last night."

"What do you mean?" I said, annoyed. "What has it got to do with him, how late I stay up?"

He opened my door for me and ignored my temper. "I'd have tried to get you to come down earlier myself, but I knew that any attempt of mine in that direction would have resulted in your staying up later still.

Anyway, you shouldn't have to be told. You know your nerves have been under a terrific strain. You simply must take it easy."

I almost stamped my foot. "I don't see why it's any affair of yours." I was furious, because I knew my voice was trembling. I added with as much cold dignity as I could command, "Good night."

I started to close the door, but he put his foot in it and pushed his way in.

I fell back and said with helpless anger, "Will you kindly—"

"Yes, I know—get out—but the answer is no. I'm going to lock up in here first."

"I don't want your protection," I declared, on the verge of tears.

"I know. The pleasure's all mine."

He searched the place, locked the door and fixed the window. Then he turned to me and regarded me coolly. "Have a good sleep and don't worry about anything. No one can get in."

I stood looking at him and holding onto a chair. I felt wretchedly ill—my head ached violently, and the room seemed to be spinning a little—but I did not want him to know it. I was waiting for him to go through into his own room, so that I could tear off my clothes and fall onto the bed.

He turned to go and then stopped and came back. He looked at me oddly for a moment and then said in a low voice, "Have you ever noticed matches lying outside your door?"

"Matches!" I repeated in amazement.

"Three matches," he said slowly, "lying in the corridor just outside the door."

"Good heavens, no!" I said. "Whatever are you talking about? Have you seen any outside my door?"

He shook his head. "But they were outside mine one night. The night Kay was murdered. I didn't think much of it at the time—except that they lay so evenly, side by side."

He said good night then and went off to his own cabin.

As I undressed I remembered Lady Marsh and her three matches, but I could not think of any explanation and felt too ill to try.

I was not quite asleep when I heard someone come into Robert's cabin, and instantly I was wide awake again.

I heard them talking in low voices and recognized Mr. Ogilvie as the visitor. A moment later someone else came into the room, and I heard the clink of glasses.

My interest deepened, and I strained my ears to hear.

The third person went out again, and Robert and Mr. Ogilvie came close to the door, so that I could hear something of what was said.

Mr. Ogilvie stated, "Well, they're all here and labeled. If there is anything in this we ought to find out something."

Robert's reply was indistinguishable, and though I scarcely breathed, in my effort to hear, I could not make out what they were doing.

Suddenly there was a small crash and the tinkling sound of broken glass. Mr. Ogilvie let out a few strong oaths and seemed to be in a violent temper about it, but Robert laughed. "What does it matter?" he said. "We can always get that again tomorrow."

"But it's the time, man . . ." and something else that I could not hear.

Robert laughed again. "Don't break any more then. Come on, let's get on with these."

They fell silent then, with only an occasional exclamation and, every now and then, the faint tinkle of glass.

I could not figure it out and began to lose interest and to get sleepy again. And then suddenly it hit me. Of course! They were doing the fingerprints! They had somehow got them on glasses—probably from the dining saloon. It would be easy enough if the stewards were instructed about it.

I was wide awake again and listening for the denouement, but if it ever came I did not hear it. The tinkling noises went on and on, and I went to sleep at last in spite of myself. I dreamed that I was looking through endless glasses for one I wanted, but I could not find it.

CHAPTER THIRTY-TWO

I FELT MUCH BETTER the next morning. I went up on deck and felt so healthy that I actually got Chet to play a game of deck tennis with me. He won, of course, and after it was over he came around and gave me a lot of pointers which he said would improve my game no end.

I asked him if he had heard the crying again last night after he had gone back to bed. He seemed a bit embarrassed and replied briefly that he had not. He went off rather abruptly, and I realized that, although he had selected me as his confidante, when he happened to be in the mood, I must not presume by touching on the subject when he was not.

I walked over to the rail and, resting my arms on it, gazed down into the water. I was thinking about Chet and the ghostly crying when I became conscious that someone was standing beside me. I did not look up but decided that whoever it was would make a remark about the weather soon enough.

"Carla?" Robert said tentatively.

I kept my eyes on the water. "Either it's a whale," I murmured, "or Mrs. Jennings has lost her knitting bag overboard. If it's a whale I suppose we ought to try and harpoon it or something, because I believe they're valuable—especially if they get sick at their stomachs and—have to put up. Only it isn't the whale that's valuable in that case, it's—"

He said, "Carla!" again, more firmly, at that point, and I raised my head and looked at him for the first time.

"Oh, hello," I said carelessly.

He stared at the horizon for a while without answering, and then he said, "I'd like you to do something for me if you will. I want you to talk to Mrs. Jennings and get all the gossip you can about everybody on board. She must know all their private affairs by now, and if you can get her to talk it might help me to put the pieces together. I'd do it myself, but I've annoyed her on several occasions, and she's stopped saying even so much as good morning to me."

"I suppose I could," I said doubtfully. "Only I always get sleepy when she starts to talk to me. Don't you think someone else could do it better?"

He said quickly, "No, no one but you could do it properly. I'd be very much obliged if you would."

I tried not to feel pleased because he had asked me to help him, and said carelessly, "All right, I'll do what I can. By the way, how did the fingerprint test come out?"

Somehow, without moving, he seemed to withdraw from me at that. He said, quite courteously, but with a definite finality, "I'd rather not say anything about it just now. It isn't quite complete, and I don't want to make any mistakes."

I felt chilled and hurt and said coldly, "Oh."

"I'm sorry I can't tell you any more. I shall when I can."

"It doesn't matter at all," I said indifferently. "Well, I guess I'll go and get Mrs. Jennings off my chest before lunch. Bye." I walked off, leaving him leaning on the rail and staring rather somberly before him.

I was rather pleased with the way I had treated him. It seemed to me that I had struck just the right note of amiable indifference—the perfect treatment for a philanderer.

I tracked Mrs. Jennings down in the drawing room. She was crocheting this time on an evil-looking thing that was made up of purple, green and orange squares so far.

"Isn't it a lovely day?" I inquired, getting in ahead of her.

She took me up with enthusiasm and said, "Yes, isn't it?"

I dropped into a chair near her and fingered the woolen abomination that dangled from her needle.

"Looks interesting," I said brightly. "What's it going to be?"

"An afghan. For my daughter's hope chest."

"It's very pretty," I lied. "Tell me about your daughter. I've seen the pretty things you are making for her, but you've never told me anything about her."

Well, I'd asked for it, of course, and there was nothing I could do but sit back and try to keep my mind from wandering while she served her daughter up from the time of conception—I suppose modesty prevented her from going back any further than that—up until the day Gertrude had waved good-by to her from the pier at Sydney. I squirmed and twisted in my chair, swallowed yawns until my eyes watered and waited wearily for a chance to steer her off.

It came when she finally mentioned Gertrude's beautiful singing voice.

I insinuated quickly, "I hear Lucy Marsh has a lovely voice too."

Mrs. Jennings snorted. "Lucy Marsh! Do you know, they've spent literally thousands on that girl's voice, and nothing has ever come of it. Nothing ever will either. They're trying to marry her off now. They say she has an attractive beau at home who wants to marry her, but they're taking her on this trip to see if something better will turn up. If nothing does they'll marry her to this man."

"What are they going to do with Phyllis?" I asked.

"The Lord only knows," she said, shaking her head. "They're not bothering about Phyllis yet—they have enough on their hands with Lucy. When they get her settled I suppose they'll start on Phyllis. Having daughters was a great disappointment to them—they wanted sons."

"I don't see why they couldn't think of both the girls at the same time," I said. "Seems a bit hard on Phyllis."

"Well, but daughters are a problem," Mrs. Jennings said seriously. "I know my Gertrude is very picky about the men who come to see her. She's had so many beaux, you know, but she's so particular. I tell her that you can't expect to find a perfect man—it's better just to take a man who'll make a good husband. You—"

Feeling that if I never heard about Gertrude again it would be too soon, I interrupted hastily.

"What kind of people are Sir Alfred and Lady Marsh?" I asked bluntly.

"Common," said Mrs. Jennings promptly. "He got his knighthood through politics, and he was only the figurehead, doing as he was told. As for her, she was the daughter of a country grocer who had some money. Her chief concern now is to crash society."

"What society?" I asked unthinkingly.

She seemed a bit confused and after several false starts finally explained, "Well, of course she wants to become intimate with the best people."

"Oh yes," I said, pretending to understand because I wanted to change the course.

I cleared my throat and suggested, "Don't you think Celia Merton is a bit that way too?"

"Oh, dear me, no, not at all—no, no, no, indeed. Celia is a lady."

I was a bit surprised and said, "Oh," very meekly.

"Celia," she announced, "is one of the few ladies left," and looked at me severely for a moment.

"She seems a nice girl," I admitted docilely.

"Girl?" Mrs. Jennings raised her eyebrows. "I happen to know she's thirty-eight."

"But that's not old these days."

Somewhat to my surprise, she veered round and agreed with me. "No, it's not," she said brightly. "Not really, when you come to think of it. Now Gertrude—" She stopped suddenly and fell to counting stitches, and I realized that I was not to know Gertrude's age after all.

"I wonder if Celia has ever had a trip like this before?" I prodded gently.

She said at once, "Oh no. This is her big trip. She wanted to meet someone and get married. She told me she had saved and pinched for years to be able to take the trip and get the clothes to wear for it."

I said, "Hum," thinking of Celia's clothes and wishing I could have been with her to help her select them when she bought them.

The old fountain continued to spout. "Celia, you know, comes of very fine American stock. Her ancestors came over in the Mayflower."

I tried to look impressed and murmured, "Really?"

"Oh yes. Now *my* ancestors—"

"But how did she get into teaching?" I broke in quickly.

"Well, her parents were wealthy at one time, but they lost all their money, and poor Celia had to do something. Of course she chose teaching, as a lady usually does. My daughter would teach if she had to, but it isn't necessary, so—"

"Why didn't you bring your daughter with you on this trip?" I asked, thinking that perhaps if I got too personal she might shut up about her daughter and herself.

She actually colored, and I could see that I had happily touched on a sore spot.

"Oh well, she thought she'd stay at home. We—er—didn't know Mr. Imhoff was going until shortly before he sailed—he kept it a secret." She worked the crochet needle furiously for a space and then settled down into a confidential tone. "You see, Mr. Imhoff has been visiting us regularly for years, and of course we thought—I know my daughter has turned down several men because of him—my husband, you know, is on the board of directors of his school, and—well, when I heard he was going on this trip I thought I'd go too. I've always wanted to go on a trip, but the captain is so busy, it's hard for him to get away, so I thought since Mr. Imhoff was going I'd just go along, too, as a lady traveling quite without friends is at such a disadvantage. I asked Gertrude if she wanted to come, but she was afraid Mr. Imhoff might think she was running after him."

"Oh yes," I said, carefully keeping my face composed. "I see. That's true. You can never tell about men—he might get that idea."

"Yes. And of course she has never run after a man in her life."

"No, indeed," I murmured.

So the old hellcat was treading on Mr. Imhoff's heels wherever he went to see that he didn't pick up with another woman. I reflected that he must have kicked over the traces to some extent when he went ashore at Tahiti with Kay.

And no wonder the affair of the scarf had upset him so. He had to consider Mrs. Jennings' strict ideas of propriety, the fact that her husband was on the board of directors, and his pension. I understood why Mrs. Jennings had been looking so smug and contented recently. Mr. Imhoff would have to marry dear old Gertrude now.

I realized with a start that she had been talking, and I hadn't heard what she was saying. She finished earnestly, "Wouldn't you?"

I apologized and asked her to repeat it.

She gave me a slightly fishy look. "I *said*, I thought I'd ask Mr. Imhoff his intentions in regard to my daughter, because there is no use in her turning down man after man if this isn't going to come to anything. I know he's very fond of her, of course, but some men are afraid of marriage. Wouldn't you ask him?"

"Certainly," I said recklessly, not wishing to cross her.

"Then you'll excuse me, I know." She gathered up the afghan—now looking like a cross section of the funny papers—and got to her feet. "He always takes his constitutional before lunch; I'll walk with him."

I spared a moment of pity for Mr. Imhoff as she went off, and then yawned and reflected idly that I'd need another session with her, since I hadn't yet touched on Chet or Peter, nor, for that matter, on Sally and Kay.

Celia wandered up and dropped into a chair near me. She blinked, yawned and then laughed at herself and explained, "I'm sleepy. I didn't get much sleep last night." She thought for a moment and then frowned faintly and became more serious. "You know, every now and then I can hear some girl crying in our part of the ship."

CHAPTER THIRTY-THREE

A SLOW, UNPLEASANT CHILL seemed to spread along my spine. I stared at Celia and then asked anxiously, "When do you hear it? And where, exactly?"

She seemed vague and not particularly interested. "Oh, at night, sometimes. Somewhere near my cabin."

"Can you hear it from inside your cabin?"

"No, but out in the corridor, near my cabin."

Lucy came up just then and said that lunch was ready, and they went off together. Lucy had nodded to me briefly—she hadn't been any too cordial to me of late.

I felt depressed and uneasy when they had gone. I didn't believe in ghosts of course, but I had seen that hateful grey mist thing myself—and now this weird crying in the night. I suddenly decided to go and tell Robert all about it, even if we were mad at each other. I didn't want to tell Mr. Ogilvie. I knew he'd look at me suspiciously and then ask innumerable questions, not only of me, but of Chet and Celia as well.

I found Robert on one of the lower decks, talking to the captain. The captain had kept pretty much in the background since the murders, and I noticed that he looked pretty bad. As I came up he nodded to me and went off. I told Robert about Chet and Celia and the crying, and he listened with deep attention. When I had finished he asked me to go along with him to that section of the ship while he looked around.

I refused absentmindedly, my head in a whirl. I had caught Robert's last few words to the captain, and he had said, "There was only one set of fingerprints on the bottle—and they were Sally's."

I looked after him as he went off, and my hair positively stood on end.

I shook my head and put my mind firmly on Mrs. Jennings. I decided to engage her again immediately after lunch. I discovered, however, that she always took a nap, so I took a book along and stationed myself in the drawing room, determined to trap her when she came up for tea.

She appeared at four o'clock, and the look she gave me was very fishy indeed. I felt, somehow, like an intruder in someone else's house.

She seemed to smell a rat too. She said, "Well, young lady, I've seen a lot of you today. What has happened to your usual friends?"

I thought furiously and used the interval to smooth my dress deco-
rously over my knees. "I'm tired of them," I said at last. "Smoking and
drinking—and nothing but dirty jokes. I'd like some clean talk for a
change."

It seemed to go down pretty well. She almost smirked and said, "Well,
you've come to the right person, young lady."

"I know. I think if poor Sally had only realized—"

"You're right," said Mrs. Jennings emphatically. "But the poor child
had no chance, none whatever. As far as I can make out a colored chauffeur did duty for her mother."

I shook my head and said "Tch, tch. Not really?"

"Yes. You know her parents were divorced, and neither of them actually wanted Sally—although she was awarded to the mother. It would
have been better, I think, if she had been awarded to an orphan asylum.
The mother had a violent temper, and no servant would stay with her
except this colored chauffeur. He was with her for years, and for stretches
at a time he was the only servant. She used to go off on trips and leave
him in charge of Sally. He was kind enough, I believe, but of course as
the child grew older she did pretty much as she liked. She knew he was
only a servant after all. Her mother hardly saw her and simply handed
her whatever money she wanted so that she need not be bothered with
her."

"It's a shame," I said musingly. "You know, it's a pity Sally didn't take
more notice of Chet. He's a nice boy."

She said yes with something of doubt in her voice. "His family is
quite well to do. But they've had their troubles with Chet. As a matter of
fact, he ran off and got married when he was seventeen. They had it
annulled. Now they've sent him off on this trip a bit earlier than they
had intended, in order to get him away from some older woman who
was taking up all his time. He's woman mad, I'm afraid."

"Well—but then, he'll meet plenty of women on a trip like this.
He'll probably go back thoroughly involved all over again."

She shook her head sadly and murmured, "His poor family."

I wanted to get her around to Peter or Kay Bayliss. After a moment's
quick thinking I said, "You'd think, to look at them, that Peter would be
much more that kind than Chet."

"Peter Condit!" she almost shouted. "That one! No woman is safe
near him—no woman at all."

I thought with some amusement that she'd gone wide of the mark
there. I knew perfectly well that Peter was very particular about his
women, and those he considered outside the pale—a large majority—
would be quite safe with him.

A steward brought us some tea, and Mrs. Jennings poured with great dignity. When she was sipping comfortably I started her off again.

"At least Peter hasn't been married," I suggested tentatively.

She raised her eyebrows, and said, "Hmm. As a matter of fact, he has no money, none at all, and he would be only too pleased to marry a rich woman. This trip was a windfall for him—dead uncle, you know. He's using every penny of it, too, instead of putting it in the bank against the future."

"Perhaps he considers it an investment. If he finds a rich woman and marries her it will have been worth his while."

"There are no rich women on this boat," she said decisively.

I wondered how she knew that I was not a rich woman. I had a deluxe cabin, and I knew that my clothes looked like it. I came to the conclusion that she must know all about me as she seemed to know all about the others. I decided with sudden eagerness to find out what she knew about Robert.

"There's a rich man on board though," I said and tried to laugh naturally.

"Two," she said, nodding. "Sir Alfred and Mr. Arnold."

I tried to sound innocently surprised. "I didn't know that Mr. Arnold was rich."

"Oh yes, certainly. He has a deluxe cabin."

"Well, I'm not rich, and I have one too."

"Well, but in your case it's different. The money was put aside for the trip, and I can see your uncle's point in getting deluxe accommodations for you—a young girl traveling alone."

My mouth fell open a little, and I began to wonder if she was a mind reader.

"As for Mr. Arnold," she went on, "he definitely has the money—perfume business—makes plenty. And his sister—well, do you know who his sister is?"

"No," I whispered and leaned closer.

"His sister . . ." She breathed a name into my ear that caused me to sit up straight, my eyes flying wide open. The case had been in the papers—a very unsavory divorce, the couple rich and socially prominent. There were three children, I recalled.

"Then," I said, trying to keep my voice steady and casual, "that was his sister and her three children seeing him off at Tahiti."

She nodded. "But of course he's trying to keep it quiet. He got her out to Tahiti somehow, without anyone getting wind of it, and he wants to keep her there for a year or more until the thing dies down."

"Has he ever been married himself?" I asked recklessly.

"No, but he's had several affairs. There was one with a notorious poetess in San Francisco."

"Is it—still flourishing?"

"No. It was broken up about a year ago."

I said, "Tch, tch," rather vaguely, and she glanced at me and observed, "It *is* awful, isn't it? The goings on, I mean. I often wonder what we're all coming to."

"You're quite right," I said falsely—because I didn't care, and never have, what the world's coming to. "I often wonder about poor Kay—what her history was and all that. She certainly kept her private affairs to herself. I never knew anything about her beyond the fact that she was married to a man named Bayliss who died and left her a widow."

She took it up for me from there. "He didn't leave much money either. Kay was in much the same position as Peter—she was looking for a rich husband. That's why she was spending the last nickel of Bayliss' insurance on this trip. She'd had three tries at making money out of marriage—and failed every time. Her first was well dressed, with the manners of a gentleman, and she thought he had money. As it turned out, he didn't have a penny and had married her because he thought she had it. That ended in divorce. I believe she was in love with the next one. He was a song writer and always expecting to make a fortune out of his next song. She married him on the expectation, but after four years she fell out of love with him and decided that the fortune was not forthcoming. She divorced him, and he made his fortune the next year, but he was too angry with her to give her any, and besides, she had already married Bayliss. Bayliss was older and spent money like water. As a matter of fact, he got it at the races—and spent it there too. He died suddenly and left nothing whatever but this five-thousand-dollar insurance policy. He'd bought it when he was drunk and only kept it up because the man who sold it to him was a friend of his."

She paused for breath and then added a summary. "Such people! I can't comprehend it."

I thought it over in silence for a while and came to the conclusion that I had been doing Mrs. Jennings an injustice when I called her a boring old fool. Old fool she might be, but she was far from boring.

But she was talking again, and I came to attention in time to hear her say, ". . . do you think you could guess?"

I shook my head.

She folded up her knitting, drew in her chin and said in a voice of triumph, "Peter Condit."

"Peter Condit?" I said helplessly.

"Yes, Peter Condit."

"Peter Condit what?" I asked desperately.

"What?"

"What about Peter Condit?"

She stuffed the knitting into her bag and got to her feet, looking offended. She started off and threw over her shoulder, "Kay Bayliss' first husband, of course."

CHAPTER THIRTY-FOUR

I SAT STILL for a while and thought that over. It did not seem possible somehow. Kay and Peter. They had always been friendly, and that was all. But then, I supposed, Peter would be friendly to any ex-wife of his—provided she were witty and amusing and sophisticated. I came to the conclusion, with a shake of my head, that it must be true anyway, because Mrs. Jennings knew everything about everybody.

The sun was setting, and I realized with sudden uneasiness that the drawing room was growing dim and shadowy. I got up in a mild panic and hurried to the door. I thought I heard a rustling behind me, but I was too frightened to turn around and look. I raced out onto the deck and gave a little gasp of relief when I found Mr. Imhoff there, stretched out in his deck chair, reading a book.

I hesitated for a moment and then walked to the drawing-room windows and peered in. The place seemed to be deserted, but I noticed that a handkerchief lay on the floor beside a deep armchair. It was at about the spot where I thought I had heard the rustling.

Robert came up as I stood there and asked quizzically, "What are you looking for?"

I forgot to be cold and said in the voice of a conspirator, "See that handkerchief on the floor in there?"

"Yes. Are you going to make it disappear?"

"Go in and get it," I whispered. "I'll explain when you bring it out."

He went off without a word, and the next minute I saw him walk across and pick it up. He came out holding it in his hand.

There was a trace of the old twinkle in his eye as he handed it to me. "It's a long voyage, I know," he said seriously, "and the laundry facilities are not up to much, but I can always lend you one or two if you're as desperate as this."

"Listen, will you!" I said impatiently. "I think it belongs to someone who was hiding in a chair and listening to Mrs. Jennings and me chatting about everybody's private affairs."

He took it back then and looked it over carefully. It was a cheap white handkerchief. It had no monogram but seemed too large for a woman's and too small to be a man's.

"Could this size be used by a woman as well as a man?" he asked curiously.

"It could," I said doubtfully. "Especially if she had a cold."

He put it in his pocket and took my arm companionably. "Let's go and dress for dinner, and you can tell me what Mrs. Jennings said over a cocktail."

I went down with him, and while I was dressing I reviewed my treatment of him with satisfaction. I felt I was taking him with casual dignity, and it seemed to be about right. He had come in with me and looked around briefly before going through the connecting door to his own room, and I had left him to it while I busied myself turning on the bath.

I dressed quickly and went on up to the smoke room, although I could hear Robert still fooling around in his own cabin. I knew he would have preferred that I wait for him, so that we could sit together while I told him all the gossip, but I decided that I would make it a little harder for him to get me alone than he had anticipated.

Peter was sitting alone with the inevitable drink, and Lucy and Phyllis were at another table with their before-dinner cocktails—one each and no more—in front of them.

I joined Peter, and he ordered a cocktail for me. I looked at him, with the story about Kay fresh in my mind, and wondered anew. It did not seem possible that he had ever been married to anyone.

I started to talk to him, but I noticed almost at once that he was not in his usual form. I began to watch him more closely and saw that he was drinking fast, which was quite unlike him. His usual procedure was to drink slowly and often—and he never seemed to get drunk.

A few minutes later he amazed me completely. He turned his head and gave Lucy a long stare, then raised his voice and called "Lucy! Come over here and have a cocktail with me."

Lucy colored, got up in a flutter and sat down at our table with a silly giggle. Phyllis remained where she was.

I was too astounded to do anything but sit and gape. Peter, who had scorned the Marsh girls utterly—whenever he deigned to notice them at all!

Lucy did most of the talking. With an excited rush of New Zealand accent she recited innumerable anecdotes of friends and relatives. I merely looked at her. Peter placed a careful "Really?" and a polite "How extraordinary!" at the right places.

Robert appeared after a while and took us in at a glance. He made for our table and called cheerfully, "Why are you sitting all alone, Phyllis? Come on and join the party."

She smiled and came over, bringing her drink along. He placed a chair for her beside me and seated himself between her and Lucy. I wondered if he thought he was paying me back for having come up ahead of him and joined Peter instead of waiting so that I could tell him the dirt.

The talk babbled on, and I presently discovered that I was being left out completely. Peter was giving all his attention to Lucy, and Robert was laughing and joking with both girls. Peter was pretty drunk. His speech was thick, and his natural wit was entirely gone. Twice he told Lucy that she had beautiful eyes.

I sat there, completely at sea, until the thing suddenly hit me with a blinking light. The rich match of course! Lucy and Phyllis would be Peter's last chance on this trip, and he had evidently decided on Lucy. He could pay her some attention, make a date to see her in New York, a letter or two, and the thing would be done. If not that, then he would have to go back to his friends with no money, and things would be the same as before. According to Mrs. Jennings, Lucy was not rich in her own right, but Sir Alfred was, and Sir Alfred was anxious to see Lucy married. I laughed to myself a little as I thought of Peter getting drunk in order to nerve himself to start operations.

I glanced up to find Robert looking at me oddly. He said, almost in an aside, "I'd give a lot to know what you're thinking."

"Not for sale," I said shortly and stood up. "I'm going down to dinner."

They all got up, and we trailed down to the dining saloon, Peter hanging grimly onto Lucy's arm, his face a mask of gloom.

Chet and Dr. Barton were deep in conversation as I approached my table. They stopped talking abruptly and rose as one man when they saw me. I sat down and raised my eyebrows at them.

"What's it all about?"

Chet looked confused and said, "Eh?"

"The—chin-wagging, you know. Secrets? Boyish confidences?"

Chet looked more uncomfortable than ever. "Oh, it wasn't anything. I was just telling the doc some of my theories."

"Well, let's hear them."

"Oh no, it was nothing. Nothing important."

"You must have been suspecting me then," I said, trying to be funny.

Dr. Barton laughed obligingly, but to my surprise Chet looked acutely embarrassed. I had hit upon the truth then, and it gave me a nasty jar to realize that anybody could suspect me of all that horror.

I came to Chet's rescue by saying indifferently, "It doesn't matter. Let's talk of something else."

The conversation didn't flourish, however, and I got through the meal as quickly as I could and went up to the smoke room for a liqueur.

It occurred to me that I was getting into regular liquor habits, and I got quite gloomy over my drink, thinking about how alcohol killed the white corpuscles, or something of the sort. I made a resolution to stop drinking, except at parties, when I got home—if I ever did get home. I remembered the two nights I still had to spend in my cabin and finished the liqueur at one gulp.

Robert appeared at the door, crossed the room at a rapid stride and sat down beside me on the couch.

"Tell me now," he said in a low voice. "We haven't much time."

I started to repeat all Mrs. Jennings' confidences, but halfway through we heard voices in the corridor, and he pulled me up from the couch and steered me out onto the deck. I had to finish the yarn hanging over the rail and trying to keep my teeth from chattering with cold. I got a bit mixed towards the end and nearly told him what I'd heard about himself but I managed to stop in time.

He was silent for some time after I had finished, and at last he said slowly, "Thank you very much, Carla. You've helped considerably. We'll have to go back inside now—but I want you to promise me that you won't attempt to go down to your cabin tonight without me."

I shrugged and said flippantly, "Maybe not."

CHAPTER THIRTY-FIVE

MRS. JENNINGS WAS SITTING in the corridor close to the smoke room, knitting busily. She would not go in the smoke room, of course, and I felt that I could not blame her for not wanting to sit in that empty drawing room.

She looked up as we passed her and said solemnly, "Mr. Arnold, we are all playing with fire. There's going to be another death on this ship before she docks."

I drew in my breath sharply. Robert stopped and said soothingly, "Now, Mrs. Jennings, you mustn't be nervous. I'm sure everything is going to be all right. You're careful to lock your cabin door at night?"

"Oh, I'm taking every precaution," she said, rattling her needles, "but I feel it in my bones."

We went on into the smoke room. Peter was sitting on a couch with Lucy close beside him, and Chet and Phyllis were in chairs facing them.

I suddenly felt glad that the Marsh girls had got a break—their faces were so alive and happy. Any unattractive man can find a woman, but an unattractive woman has a hard time of it. I decided that Lucy and Phyllis were probably enjoying themselves more than they ever had in their lives before.

Robert joined them, and I went over to Celia, who was sitting alone.

I noticed Mr. Imhoff—by himself and apparently sunk in gloom. Sir Alfred and Lady Marsh were at a small table, Lady Marsh talking to her husband in a steady undertone. His eyes had a faraway look in them, and I could not tell whether he was listening or not.

I talked to Celia for a while and then found myself getting bored, so I suggested a game of bridge. She was amiably willing, and when I approached Sir Alfred and Lady Marsh they accepted at once.

We settled down at a table, and I made a secret vow never to play bridge again when the voyage was over. I did it only to take my mind off the horror, and at best it was a poor makeshift.

Mr. Imhoff left shortly after we started to play. The rest of them were laughing and talking at a great rate, with Lucy's shrill voice sounding more often as she gained confidence.

Lady Marsh kept looking over at them with a pleased expression on her face. Once she bubbled right over and said archly, "Lucy and Phyllis seem to have stolen your beaux, Miss Bray. Bad girls—I must speak to them."

I laughed. I couldn't help it.

Celia spoke up rather hotly and said, "Why, no, Lady Marsh. It's just that Carla prefers playing bridge."

I thought, "Mrs. Jennings is right. Celia is a lady."

After a time, when I became dummy, I went out onto the deck for a breath of fresh air. Celia was a slow player, and her painful concentration made me restless.

The nights were no longer warm and languorous, now that we were nearing San Francisco, and I shivered as I leaned on the rail and drew my coat closer about me.

The door opened abruptly behind me, and Robert stepped out and joined me.

"Oh—hello," I said flatly.

"Hello."

He rested his arms on the rail, and we stood side by side in silence, until I announced formally that I had to go back to my bridge.

He gave a little bow and said mockingly, "And I to my gay party."

"Your . . . ?"

"Gay party," he repeated gravely. "We're being awfully jolly in there."

I laughed, but I would not look at him as we went in.

Sir Alfred was dealing a new hand, and Celia looked up and said happily, "I made it."

"Good." I sat down and saw Robert rejoin his "gay party" out of the corner of my eyes.

"What were you and Mr. Arnold doing out on deck?" Lady Marsh asked crudely.

I looked at her and saw that her face was dark with suspicion.

I picked up my hand and started to sort it. "Oh, we just went out for a little kiss."

Celia gasped, and I winked at her.

Lady Marsh had the grace to flush. "Oh, come now," she said defensively, "you know I didn't mean that."

I flicked her a glance and said, "I pass," and since it wasn't my turn she removed her attention from the deck episode and extracted the full penalty from me.

It was about an hour later that I slipped out on the deck again, only to have Robert appear beside me at once.

I turned to face him and demanded, "What is this?"

"I can't let you roam around alone. I don't want you to be alone anywhere."

I stared out into the darkness and said after a minute, "Do you mean I'm in danger?"

"What do *you* think?" he asked with a faint impatience.

He was right of course. I shivered and caught my lip firmly between my teeth.

I thought it over for a while and then said politely, "I don't like to trouble you this way though. I think I'd better go to Mr. Ogilvie and ask for a bodyguard of some sort. Maybe one of the stewards. They can't be very busy with such a small passenger list."

He leaned against the rail, his white shirt front gleaming and his face in the shadow. "You needn't bother," he said quietly. "I'm going to bodyguard you anyway."

That left me a little at a loss. I did not know whether to thank him or to tell him to go and fly his kite. Lady Marsh saved me the necessity of a decision by coming to the door and informing me, rather acidly, that they were waiting for me. She gave Robert a look of reproach as he passed. I wondered whether it was because he was being unfaithful to Lucy or to her.

The bridge game droned on. I did not go out on the deck again, having consideration for the wear and tear on Robert.

At about twelve o'clock there was a small commotion in the other group. Peter passed out completely and had to be carried downstairs by a couple of stewards.

Chet and Phyllis went off to bed shortly afterwards, going down together to keep each other company. Lucy and Robert stayed on.

The bridge ended with a bang at half-past twelve. Lady Marsh bid and made a grand slam, and as that was the rubber and they were up a tidy little sum, she suggested that we stop.

Celia and I agreed, and as we got up to go we heard a door slam somewhere.

Sir Alfred said, "Wind blowing up. Expect we're in for a bit of a storm."

I think we all had the same thought. A storm might delay us—and we would resent bitterly even so much as an extra hour on that dreadful ship.

We went down the stairs, silent and depressed. We said good night briefly, and Robert and I turned down our corridor.

He went through the routine of searching my cabin and then turned to me, but I averted my face and said, "Thank you. Good night."

He murmured, "Good night," and went through into his own cabin.

I had a silly impulse to cry after he had gone. I somehow felt sure that he had been going to kiss me. But I told myself angrily that I was not going to be one of the many that he kissed.

"He can kiss Lucy's buck teeth if he wants to," I thought hotly, "but my lipstick comes from Paris, and I'll reserve it for someone who can appreciate it."

I undressed quickly and went to bed. The boat was pitching a bit, and the wind was rising. It howled along the deck outside my window and kept me awake until I put a blanket over my head, when I drifted into an uneasy sleep.

I suppose I slept for some hours. I know I dreamed furiously—not exactly nightmares, but they gave me the sense of rushing around madly that I had had when I took gas to have a tooth extracted.

I awoke suddenly. The wind had risen to a wild shriek, and the boat was lurching drunkenly. I lay still for a while, trying to get to sleep again. Then suddenly I sat bolt upright, my ears strained and my breath coming faster. I had heard a human voice.

For a while there was nothing but the wind, and then it came again—a sobbing cry that was drowned out when the wind rose. It seemed to come from just outside my door.

I lay rigid, thinking of Sally's fingerprints on my bottle of smelling salts, and I had a confused, terrified feeling that it was no use—the thing would get right through the locked door, and I would not be able to get away.

The cry stopped, and after a while I gritted my teeth and scrambled out of bed and made for the door leading to Robert's room. Halfway across, a movement at the window caught my eye, and I turned my head sharply. As I stared that grey, faceless thing appeared there and seemed to be looking in.

I heard myself moan dully—and the next instant it was gone.

I ran to the connecting door, flung it open and stumbled through into Robert's room. I called to him frantically, but there was no answer, and after a dazed search, during which I failed to find the light switch, I realized that he was not there and that I was alone.

CHAPTER THIRTY-SIX

I COULD NOT GO BACK into my own dreadful cabin, nor could I face the shadowy emptiness of the corridor outside. I backed up against the wardrobe, shivering with cold and whimpering with fear. I had a desperate conviction that if Robert did not come the grey thing would slip in and get me.

Above the noise of the wind I heard firm steps along the corridor, and I stiffened, waiting, my eyes in the general direction of the door.

The footsteps stopped at the door, and in the gloom I could see it swing in. I called wildly, "Robert! Robert!" and the next instant I was in his arms, sobbing childishly against his shoulder.

He spoke to me gently and reassuringly and tenderly smoothed my disordered hair away from my face. For a few minutes I clung to him as though I could never let go. Then as my fear died down I became conscious of the fact that I wore nothing but a thin silk nightgown.

I backed away in some confusion, mopping at my wet eyes with Robert's handkerchief. "I—I must get a dressing gown."

He switched on the light and said, "Never mind. I have one for you."

He pulled a handsome silk garment from the wardrobe and wrapped it around me. It went around almost twice, and the sleeves dangled incongruously over my hands. I flopped them helplessly and looked up at him in some embarrassment.

"It could do with a tuck or two," he smiled, "but the color suits you beautiful. I was keeping it for my wedding night."

I sank into the wicker armchair, because my legs had gone wobbly. "I won't go back in there," I said childishly, "and you—you mustn't leave me. I'll scream horribly if you do."

He laughed and sat down on the side of the bed. "Can't seem to make up your mind, can you? Either you're ordering me to leave you alone, or—"

"Where did you go?" I said hastily.

"Out into the corridor. I thought I heard something. What frightened you?"

I told him the tale, and he got up and began to walk restlessly about the room.

"Damn it!" he said after a while. "I must have got there just too late. I heard the crying, too, and decided to go out and investigate. Whoever it was heard me coming, I suppose, and ran out onto the deck. By the time I got out it had gone."

"Do you know what it's—what's going on?" I asked fearfully.

"Something—not much. But I have an idea. If I could only have got out in time tonight!"

I curled up more comfortably in the chair and rested my head against the back. He lighted a cigarette and continued to pace the room abstractedly.

I wanted a cigarette, too, but didn't like to interrupt his train of thought. I grew drowsy, waiting for an opportunity, and presently slipped off to sleep.

I must have slept very soundly, for when I woke up I was lying in the bed, covered with a quilt, and the sun was shining into the room. Robert was nowhere to be seen. I stretched and gave a little sigh of relief, because the storm seemed to have petered out, and we would probably get into San Francisco on time.

I looked at the clock and saw that it was nine, and I scrambled out of bed in a hurry. The door must be unlocked if Robert had gone—and I did not want any steward raising his eyebrows at me!

I pulled the dressing gown around me, shook my hair out of my eyes—and caught sight of Robert, stretched out in the upper berth, his head propped on his arm, watching me lazily.

"Good heavens!" I gasped. "Have you been there all night?"

"What there was left of it—yes." He swung himself down and put on the other dressing gown. "Sleep well?"

"Ye-es. But I don't think—I mean, it isn't exactly conventional. Sleeping in the same cabin, you know."

"No," he said with mock gravity. "And I rely on you not to give me away. If it gets about you'll have to marry me. My mother will see to it. She has a little sawed-off shotgun—"

"She'd better get it out then," I said, going through the door into my own cabin. "I'm sure Mrs. Jennings knows all about it already."

Everybody seemed in better spirits that morning. San Francisco was only one more night away, and where the passengers would ordinarily be regretting the end of a pleasant voyage, they were gay with the anticipation of a normal, safe life again.

Walking on the deck after breakfast, I caught sight of Mrs. Jennings talking earnestly to Mr. Imhoff. He was wrapped in a rug, with a book on his lap, and he looked acutely unhappy. Mrs. Jennings was perched on the edge of the chair next to him.

As I passed by I called, "Good morning," to them. Mr. Imhoff nodded affably—but Mrs. Jennings cut me dead!

I walked on, wondering. I knew she had been a bit offended the day before when I had not listened to the denouement of her confidences and had had to ask her to repeat. But then, she was always taking little offenses about things and forgetting them the next time she saw you.

Could she know about my having spent most of the night in Robert's cabin? She had an almost miraculous knowledge of everybody's affairs, but, how could she possibly have found out about this? It interested me to such an extent that I decided to find out. I walked the deck until I saw her leave Mr. Imhoff, and then I trailed her into the drawing room.

"Now tell me," I said, sitting down in front of her. "What have I done that you should refuse to speak to me?"

She hauled her crocheting from its bag and set to work. "I don't like immoral women," she observed, apparently to the afghan.

"What makes you think I am immoral?"

She looked me straight in the eye and declared, "You spent the night in Mr. Arnold's cabin."

I sat back and gaped at her. At last I managed feebly, "Only from three-thirty on."

"The time, of course, has nothing to do with it," she said sternly.

I began to enjoy myself. I said gravely, "You should listen to my explanation before you brand me a scarlet woman."

She took it very seriously and said she was always willing to believe the best of people, if possible.

I told her the tale and ended by saying, with all the sweet, shy girlishness I could put into it, that Mr. Arnold had been a perfect gentleman.

She weighed it, pro and con, for two minutes. Then she said, "I see—yes. But you were very remiss in not having gone back to your own cabin."

"I know," I agreed dolefully. "But I was so frightened."

"It all comes," she observed, "from letting young women travel alone." She set her lips in a thin, straight line.

"How did you know?" I ventured presently. "About last night, I mean."

"I take an early walk on your deck every morning before breakfast, and I just happened to glance into Mr. Arnold's window. You were sleeping in the lower berth, and Mr. Arnold in the upper."

I realized, if she didn't, that you'd have to stop and actually poke your head in the window in order to see into the two berths. I decided that she had probably peered into both our windows every morning to see that all was well, and it wasn't until this morning that she had had success at last.

"Well, I hope you won't tell anybody about it," I said.

"Oh, dear, no—indeed not." She actually colored faintly, confirming my suspicion that she had told someone.

I changed the subject. "Did you ask Mr. Imhoff his intentions?"

"Yes, I did," she said, all enthusiasm. "And, do you know, he wants to marry my little girl."

"Oh?"

"Yes, and I'll be so busy as soon as we land. I'll have to buy all sorts of things to sew for her trousseau. And Mr. Imhoff and I are going together to buy the ring."

I said, "That's fine," and drifted off. I knew she wanted to tell me more about it, but I felt faintly disgusted and contemptuous. I thought idly that she'd probably punish me for deserting her by telling my escapade to a few more people.

I went up to the boat deck. Phyllis and Robert were standing in the shadow of a lifeboat, deep in conversation, and Lucy was sitting a little apart, reading a book. Chet and Dr. Barton were playing deck tennis. Celia was leaning against a ventilator, looking out to sea, and I went over and joined her.

"Are you looking forward to tomorrow as much as I am?" I asked her.

"Not exactly." She hesitated. "I've had a wonderful time, and although I'll be glad to get back to my teaching I wouldn't have minded the trip being longer."

"It's a pity this thing had to happen and spoil it for you," I said feelingly.

"Well, it doesn't matter to me so much. It was exciting, you know, and I'm not much afraid. As for Sally and Kay—I'm sorry, but after all, I didn't know them very well."

I remembered that Sally and Kay had never been very kind to her—had made fun of her on several occasions.

"There are two things I regret," she went on after a moment. "One was when I told you Sally's body was in the cabin next to you. It's—very hard for me to refuse anybody anything."

"Oh, forget it," I said hastily. "It doesn't matter at all. It was Peter's fault anyway. He made you think it was a joke."

"Yes," she said eagerly. "I thought it was only a joke." She paused and went on more slowly. "I thought he was getting me into your circle, and I was flattered. I know now that I was foolish. I don't belong in your kind of circle. I have my own at home; they're very nice, and I'll be glad to get back to them."

I felt confused and embarrassed and did not know quite what to say. I felt a little sorry that I had not taken more notice of her during the voyage.

"Yes," she said after a moment, "I like them, and they suit me. I'll be glad to get back to them and tell them all about it."

Mr. Imhoff passed behind us and doffed his cap.

"The old fool!" Celia murmured when he was out of earshot.

I looked at her in surprise. I had a vague idea that she'd been trying to capture him, and Mrs. Jennings had been sure that she was anxious to get married. I thought, "It isn't so; we're both wrong."

"I can never forgive myself," she said scornfully, "for agreeing to claim his miserable scarf, but he was in such a state about it. He is a complete fool—and has a great idea of his own importance."

"Mrs. Jennings tells me he is going to marry her daughter Gertrude," I said, wondering if she knew.

She threw back her head and laughed heartily. "I knew the old devil would trap him in the end," she said at last. "I'm afraid I'm sorry for them both."

I laughed, too, but the memory of Mrs. Jennings' libelous tongue made me a little indignant. I was sure now that Celia had not taken the trip for the purpose of getting married.

"By the way," I said conversationally, "have you heard that I spent the night in Robert Arnold's cabin?"

"Before eight this morning," she admitted, smiling at me. "No need to tell you who told me."

We both laughed heartily again. "Let's sit down somewhere," I suggested, "and I'll tell you all about it. I'd sew a red A on my chest, only I suppose it would look like boasting."

We found chairs, and while we were getting settled I noticed that Peter had come up and was lounging gracefully on the footrest of Lucy's chair, while she talked volubly to him. Robert and Phyllis were still deep in conversation under the lifeboat.

For the first time that morning my spirits began to droop again.

CHAPTER THIRTY-SEVEN

I REMEMBER THINKING as I sat down to lunch that day that there was only one more afternoon and only one more night to go through, and that it would not be long before we were all safely on shore. If I could only have known how many things were to happen in that short space of time!

Chet and Dr. Barton seemed in good spirits. I managed to ask Chet, while Dr. Barton was occupied with the menu, if he had heard the crying the night before. He said no and changed the subject abruptly.

Dr. Barton told us they were going to have the captain's dinner that night in spite of everything, but that they would not bother with any dancing. I was glad about the dancing. I did not feel like it at all, somehow.

Chet seemed to be yearning with his whole soul to get off the ship. It was as though he had finished with the awful experience, had put it right out of his mind and was simply marking time until he could get to America and turn his attention to something else.

Dr. Barton was rather gloomy about our landing. He looked forward to endless questioning and investigations, and he declared it was going to be an infernal nuisance and a bore. He told us that the captain was taking it very hard. He had practically retired from any social life and spent a great deal of time by himself, presumably brooding. He had ceased to take any part in the investigation and was leaving it all to Mr. Ogilvie.

I felt sorry for the captain. I supposed that the whole business would reflect on him to a certain extent, even though he was not to blame.

I went up on deck after lunch. The weather was fine and warmer than it had been the day before. I stood leaning on the rail, and I remember wondering what I could do to make the afternoon pass quickly. It was all wasted thought!

Robert came up after a while and said, "I want you to come with me and interview Peter."

"You're going to ask him about Kay?"

"No," he said with a faint smile. "You are. I want you to ask him casually why he never told us."

"But suppose he asks how I found out about it. What shall I say?"

"Tell him the truth. Just say that Mrs. Jennings told you, and let it go at that."

I nodded, and we went off to the smoke room, where we found Peter having coffee and a liqueur. He preferred having dinner twice a day rather than lunch and dinner; his breakfast was nothing but black coffee. Lucy was sitting with him, and Robert swore under his breath.

I glanced at him and was foolish enough to murmur, "Too bad—you had better look out or Peter will get Lucy away from you."

"There is always suicide," he said absently.

Lucy had coffee and a liqueur, too, and was smoking a cigarette in a long holder—and somehow looked as though she'd like to throw the three of them into the ocean.

As we sat down with them Robert pulled the cigarette from Lucy's holder and gave it to me. "You don't need it," he said to her, "and Carla always wants one when she sits down anywhere. And I haven't any on me."

Lucy giggled and said shrilly, "Well, I like that, I must say."

Peter gave us a languid, chilly stare. He drained the liqueur and asked coolly, "What is it now? I presume I'm right in supposing that Mr. Arnold would not waste his time in my company if he did not have something special to ask me."

"I did want a word with you," Robert admitted mildly. He poured Lucy's liqueur into her coffee and drank the concoction.

Lucy gave a little scream. "Why, Bob! What have I done to you, to have you treat me like this?"

"Bob," indeed! And her manner seemed to suggest that she knew Robert was jealous of Peter, but he mustn't be a naughty boy.

Robert smiled at her—kindly—but his eyes returned restlessly to Peter. "Expect our chat will have to wait."

Peter swung around in his chair and dropped his hand onto Lucy's. "Do me a favor, kitten?"

Lucy gasped, colored and murmured, "What is it?"

"Will you go down now for a nap? So that you'll be all fresh for the captain's dinner tonight."

Lucy looked a bit disappointed. "But I'm not tired," she pouted.

"That doesn't matter. I want to have cocktails with you, and I'm going to arrange to have dinner with you. You must put on your prettiest dress and feel your best, for I'm determined that this last night on board shall be perfect."

She went off like a lamb at that, and when she had disappeared Peter swung around again and faced us, curiously heavy-eyed and faintly defiant. He muttered, "So what!" as though to forestall comment, although neither of us had offered any.

Robert shrugged, and I controlled a sudden desire to laugh.

Peter ordered a brandy and then asked—still faintly defiant, "What do you want?"

Robert was silent for a moment, and when he spoke I realized that he must have decided to dispense with my services. He said simply, "I merely want the details of your marriage with Kay."

"Oh." Peter drained the brandy at one gulp. "I was wondering when you nosy sleuths would stub your toes on that."

"We know all," Robert murmured humorously.

"You wish you did."

Robert laughed and said good-naturedly, "*Touche.* But about this marriage?"

Peter took out a cigarette and began to roll it around in his fingers without lighting it. "It may sound a bit sordid to you, because you have enough money to be noble without feeling it. Anyway, at that time I was very ambitious and wanted to marry a woman of family and position. I didn't care so much about the money—then. I wanted to have influential friends so that I could make my own money. Kay had no family and no money—and she wanted to marry money. We fell in love and were young enough to decide that we had to get married. It didn't last of course. We couldn't stand each other after a while. We were both too selfish. When we parted it was amiably enough, and we scraped together some money and got a divorce. I heard of her occasionally after that, and when I got on this boat—there she was. We laughed about it and decided to say nothing to the other passengers. That's all."

He lighted the cigarette and tossed the match expertly into an ash tray that was some distance from him. "And you can't hang me for that," he added carelessly.

"Afraid not," said Robert, eyeing him thoughtfully. "We'll just have to go on groping."

Peter stood up. "If that's all I'm going down to take a sleep—keep myself fresh for tonight and Lucy."

He walked off, and I said wonderingly, "I believe he means it, for Lucy."

"Looks like it—but what matter. It'll give Lucy poise."

"She doesn't need it," I said nastily.

"I'll wash your mouth out with soap if you don't mend your manners," he said idly. "By the way, I think you might speak to Mrs. Jennings again. If anyone on this ship knows who's guilty of these two murders she should."

"Do you mean I should just go and ask her if she knows who did it?"

"Just that."

"All right," I said resignedly. "When I finish this cigarette."

Lady Marsh appeared at the door, swept the room with an eagle glance and made her way purposefully towards us.

I said, "Hello." She gave me a frozen glance—and cut me dead!

She gave Robert a cordial smile. "Mr. Condit and Chet want to dine with us tonight—make a little party, you know. You have no objections?"

"I couldn't have," said Robert blandly, "since I shan't be there."

Her face fell, and I could see that she had planned a gay little party, with all the nicest men on board at her table.

"Oh, but dear me—you're not going to spoil the party, are you? It's all planned. And we're going to have cocktails first in somebody's cabin."

He said firmly, "I'm sorry, Lady Marsh, but I have other very definite plans for the evening."

"Now you think it over—don't decide at once." And she walked off quickly before he could refuse again.

"Don't you be a Lady Marsh when you grow up, Carla," he said, smiling at me lazily.

"A thoroughly nasty woman. With so few on board she wants to make up a party and leave the odd few sitting by themselves."

I shrugged and stamped out my cigarette.

"Why did she cut you?" he asked after a moment. "I know she doesn't want you on the party, but it hardly explains the snub direct."

"It's very simple," I said indifferently. "You see, Mrs. Jennings takes a walk on our deck every morning and carefully looks in all the windows, so that by now the whole ship knows that I slept with you last night."

"So you have disgraced me," he said, shaking his head. "I thought you would the minute I laid eyes on you."

"I'm sorry," I said coldly. "If you like I'll pin up a notice in the lounge to the effect that I left you as I found you." I stood up. "I'll go and talk to Mrs. Jennings."

He bowed a trifle formally, and I went off. I decided to go down to my cabin first and freshen up a little, but when I got there I sat down on the bed and stared apathetically at nothing.

I thought of Lady Marsh and her selfishness and rudeness in leaving Celia and myself out of her party. For some reason I did not mind for myself, but I was particularly infuriated on Celia's account. Apparently Lady Marsh expected us to amuse ourselves with Mr. Imhoff, who was no longer any good to anyone and who always retired now directly after dinner.

I realized suddenly that for some time I had been looking at something that was clamoring at my brain for direct attention.

I narrowed my gaze and focused it—and felt little tendrils of fear unfolding in me.

Something grey and shimmering lay folded over the back of the wicker armchair.

CHAPTER THIRTY-EIGHT

I GAVE a frightened glance around the room and then took an uncertain step towards the thing—and recognized it.

It was my missing robe again, but it had been turned inside out. I had never connected it with the grey mist, and I wondered a little that I had never thought of it. It was a very pale blue satin on the outside, but it was lined in grey chiffon, and it had a large circular collar of grey chiffon, which hung down the back. It was very clear to me now that the grey mist horror hard been someone wearing my robe inside out and with the collar thrown over the head and face.

I rang at once for a steward and directed him to find either Mr. Ogilvie or Mr. Arnold, or both, and ask them to come to my cabin at once. I added that it was very important.

He said, "Yes, miss," wearily and went off.

Mr. Ogilvie and Robert came down shortly afterwards, and I showed them the thing.

Mr. Ogilvie was distinctly disagreeable about it. He said, "If you had only thought a little, Miss Bray, you could have told us long ago that it was your dressing gown this person was wearing."

"And what good would that have done?" I demanded, annoyed. "We knew somebody was wearing something. Unless you believe in ghosts," I added scornfully.

He didn't answer, though he looked mad enough.

Robert fingered the dressing robe and said, "Pretty trifle, isn't it? Speaking of ghosts, I had a dear old aunt—"

Mr. Ogilvie broke in fiercely. "Mr. Arnold, will you please come into your cabin? I want to speak to you for a minute."

He stamped through the connecting door, and Robert followed him, pausing to give me a grin and a wink.

I decided to speak to Mrs. Jennings and have it over with, so I went on up to the drawing room. I almost felt as though I ought to knock before entering, and I finally tiptoed in unobtrusively and slid quietly into a chair.

"How are you getting on?" I asked sweetly.

She looked at me a bit sternly and seemed to be considering whether or not she should speak to an unmarried woman who slept in men's bedrooms, but she broke down at last and told me how she was getting on for at least five minutes.

I broke in as soon as I decently could and said earnestly, "Mrs. Jennings, Mr. Ogilvie has been trying to clear up this mystery with the help of Mr. Arnold, but I don't think they've got very far. I was thinking this morning that you probably know more about it, right this minute, than they'll ever know, with all their detective work."

She straightened up, preened herself and said with dignity, "I most certainly do."

"I thought you did," I said eagerly. "I figured that, with you, it would be a matter of character analyses." I meant, of course, a matter of peeping in windows and listening at keyholes, but I thought I'd put it rather tactfully.

I had. Mrs. Jennings gave me the prettiest smile in her repertoire—which was none too good—and announced that she knew all about everything.

I clasped my hands and breathed, "Oh, dear! I suppose you're not telling anyone?"

"Certainly not Ogilvie or that busybody, Arnold," she snorted. "I'm keeping it for the authorities."

I cleared my throat and suggested tentatively, "I suppose there's no chance of you telling me—if I promise not to breathe it to a soul?"

She hesitated, her head cocked to one side, her eyes narrowed, studying me. I think she was trying to decide whether to keep me in suspense or give herself the pleasure of telling a long story. She loved to hear herself speak.

At last an idea seemed to strike her, and her face brightened. "We'll have tea together," she announced triumphantly, "and I'll tell you then."

I tried to persuade her to tell me at once, but she would not be moved. She told me to go off and walk the deck for an hour and be back in time for tea. I knew that, for the most part, she had to take her tea alone, and I suppose she grasped at the opportunity of having company.

I went out to the deck and started vaguely to walk around, as directed. I had made half a round when I remembered that, what with finding my dressing robe and all, I had not washed up since lunch. It would be pretty unthinkable, I told myself sternly, to go to tea in Mrs. Jennings' drawing room with dirty hands.

Mr. Ogilvie and Robert were still talking in Robert's room. The discussion seemed to have become more heated, and after listening vaguely for a moment I realized that they were definitely having an argument. I went straight over and laid my ear against the door.

Mr. Ogilvie was saying, "I don't care what you say—you're in love with the girl. I've seen you before on these trips, but this time you're serious, and therefore I'm convinced that you're prejudiced. I can't take your word for it. I must do something about it—it's too serious."

"All right," said Robert, "granted—but that doesn't necessarily impair my intelligence. I tell you, I'm positive. If you'll only wait for a few hours—if you disgrace her by locking her up you'll be in a hell of a spot. You must know how serious it would be to make a mistake of that sort."

"Oh, damn!" said Mr. Ogilvie, and I heard him pull the door open. "I'll wait until after tea, and that's all!"

He slammed out, but I heard Robert go out immediately after him and catch him up somewhere along the corridor, and they began talking again.

I washed my hands and freshened up my appearance mechanically. Then Robert was in love with someone on the ship—he practically admitted it. I stared into the mirror and wondered if it could possibly be myself.

But perhaps it was Lucy or Phyllis: he had given them more attention. I knew it could not be Celia. He had always been pleasant and friendly to her but never attentive. Suppose it was I. I stared into the mirror, my eyes round and frightened—then I was going to be arrested, put into irons or something dreadful. But it was probably Lucy or Phyllis; and I suddenly felt that perhaps it would not be so bad to be put in irons.

I roused myself, set my jaw resolutely and went up on deck.

It was not yet quite four, and I began resignedly to walk around. When I came to the drawing-room windows I stopped and looked in. Mrs. Jennings was still in the same chair in which I had left her, her head bent over her knitting.

I moved off restlessly and did two more rounds. It seemed to me that I did them in nothing flat, wondered crossly if the hands of my watch were stuck and knew perfectly well that they were not. I did not want to break in on her too soon, but I was painfully anxious to hear what she had to say. It might be nothing of course—possibly only a bid for importance. But if I were about to be arrested and she did know something I was vitally concerned in finding out what it was.

I looked at my watch again, sure that it must be four o'clock by now, but it was only five minutes to.

I looked down the deck wearily and decided that I simply could not walk around again. I wandered over to one of the drawing-room windows and looked in again to see if the time seemed ripe.

Mrs. Jennings head was still bent low over her knitting, and I turned away. I walked to the end window, where I could get a better look at her face, and peered in once more.

I was surprised to discover that she was not knitting at all and that her head hung so low that I could not see her face. I stood staring at her, faintly disquieted, and waiting for her to resume her knitting, but she did not stir.

I moved back, looking in every window as I passed and thinking abstractedly, "She is probably saying her prayers or communing with her soul, and I'd better not disturb her until she has finished."

Suddenly, at the middle window, I stopped short.

There was a piece of taut cord running from the back of her chair and attached to the high carved back of a chair near by.

CHAPTER THIRTY-NINE

I STOOD THERE for a few minutes with my heart in my mouth. What could it mean? It couldn't be—oh, it couldn't be another of those ghastly murders!

I forced my eyes away from the cord and immediately began to wonder if it had been an optical delusion.

I walked dazedly down the deck to the door of the drawing room, and after a moment's hesitation I stepped inside.

She looked now as though she had stopped knitting for a moment and was looking down at it.

I went a little closer, but she did not move nor look up at my approach. She was so still that I felt a cold shiver go down my back. I stood there uncertainly, half inclined to speak to her naturally and fighting an impulse to run screaming from the room.

I could not see the cord from where I stood—had never seen it very clearly. I took a step forward and said, "Mrs. Jennings," in an unnaturally loud voice.

There was no answer and no movement, and I suddenly gave way to my terror and fled from the room. The deck steward was crossing the corridor with a tray of teacups, and I gripped his arm feverishly. With my teeth chattering I asked him to go and see what was the matter with Mrs. Jennings.

He looked at me as though he thought I were crazy but set the cups down carefully on a table and went into the drawing room. I stood just outside the door and waited.

He was back almost at once. "Will you get someone to find Mr. Ogilvie right away, miss?" he asked, his voice full of restrained excitement. "I don't want to leave here until someone comes."

"Then she's—dead?"

He said yes, briefly, and walked back into the drawing room. I thought he seemed purposely uncommunicative.

I ran out onto the deck, but there was no one in sight—and there in the broad daylight I was simply terrified of that empty deck.

I hurried along to one of the smoke-room windows and looked in. To my infinite relief I saw that Robert was sitting at one of the tables, and I staggered in the door, completely winded and almost collapsing.

Robert got up and came to me quickly, and I began to jabber stupidly at him. I believe I told him for God's sake to go to the drawing room at once.

He took my shoulders firmly and shook me a little. "Stop talking," he commanded, "and calm down."

I drew a gasping breath. "But you've got to—"

He said, "Hush!" very decisively and led me to a chair. He made me sit down, lighted a cigarette himself and handed it to me. "Now don't say anything until you relax a bit."

I drew on the cigarette and felt some of the tightness go out of my body. After a moment I looked up at him and said very slowly and clearly, "I think Mrs. Jennings has been murdered. She's in the drawing room with a steward watching her, and I am supposed to be getting Mr. Ogilvie."

He sprang up and exclaimed, "Good God! It can't be!" He walked off from me a little way, his brows drawn together and his face deadly serious; then he turned abruptly and came back. "Will you stay here and not get excited, if I go?"

I looked around the room and saw Mr. Imhoff and the smoke-room steward.

"All right," I said, trying to keep my voice steady.

"Don't go away—don't move from here, whatever happens. Will you promise?"

"All right," I said again.

Robert went off, and I sat still and tried to relax.

Mr. Imhoff came over to me. "What's all the excitement about?" he asked, eyeing me curiously.

I told him what I knew, and he hurried away, with his eyes popping, to see for himself.

The smoke-room steward, who had edged himself within earshot, looked as though he'd like to run off and see, too, but evidently decided that he had better stay where he belonged.

"This is a bad trip, miss," he observed, shaking his head. "The captain now—he's in a bad way. I feel sorry for him."

"So do I," I said wearily.

Robert came back and sat down beside me. "She's dead," he said quietly. "The cord was tied around her throat, but it didn't kill her. Her head's been bashed in. Some heavy object—but I don't know what. There's nothing in the room."

I shivered and stared dully at the table in front of me. It seemed impossible that we could ever get to San Francisco and go our separate ways.

I was conscious that Robert was looking at me, and I raised my eyes.

There was sympathy and concern in his regard, and with an effort I said, "I'm all right. I'm not going to faint or anything."

"Good girl!" But his expression did not change, and after a moment he said, "We're supposed to stay here. Ogilvie is holding court right away, and—don't worry about whatever conclusion he comes to."

I raised my head sharply and stared at him. Was he warning me that I might be arrested? I suddenly felt absurdly lighthearted.

"Do you mean that I might be blamed? That they're going to hold me—or lock me up?"

He looked at me curiously. "Well, don't be so happy about it. It may not happen, you know."

I dropped my eyes and felt my face burning with sudden color.

Mr. Imhoff came back looking rather wild. It seemed to me that he should have felt nothing but relief, but he was obviously very much shocked.

Celia came in and calmly seated herself near me. She said, "Isn't it awful?" in a conventionally shocked voice.

The Marsh girls appeared together and timidly seated themselves side by side on a couch. Peter followed and stood in the middle of the floor as though undecided what to do with his body. He finally walked over to Lucy, sat down beside her rather heavily and ordered a drink.

Chet came in, looking sullen and annoyed, and sat by himself.

Lady Marsh appeared with Sir Alfred in tow. She was volubly exclaiming over the frightfulness of the situation and seemed to be enjoying herself.

For the finale Dr. Barton and Mr. Ogilvie appeared together, their faces very grave. The captain did not attend.

Mr. Ogilvie cleared his throat in preparation for the opening speech, but Lady Marsh got in ahead of him.

"Mr. Ogilvie," she said, "while all this is going on may we have our tea? Otherwise we shall miss it entirely." One gathered that it would be a major catastrophe.

Mr. Ogilvie gave her a look in which disgust was very thinly concealed. His face said as plainly as his words could have done that a request for tea, at a time like this, was inconceivable to him. However, he nodded to the smoke-room steward, who scuttled off.

He cleared his throat again then and started afresh.

"Ladies and gentlemen: As you know, another of our number has been brutally murdered. I wish to question each one of you as to your whereabouts this afternoon . . . ." He paused as though undecided how to continue.

Lady Marsh stepped into the breach and said, "Quite right," nodding her head emphatically several times. She was still enjoying herself.

Mr. Ogilvie leveled a cold stare at her and said, "Thank you, Lady Marsh. Perhaps you won't mind, then, if we begin with you."

"Not at all." She settled herself in her chair and then gave the most detailed description of half an afternoon's activities that I have ever heard, and inasmuch as she had slept for an hour after lunch I still wonder how it could possibly have taken so long to tell. After her sleep she had gone up to the boat deck and stayed there until four. She had read, written some letters and done some sewing. She had also gazed out to sea for a while. At four o'clock she had come down and had seen a small crowd around the entrance to the drawing room. Upon inquiring she had been told by a steward what had happened and had been asked to go to the smoke room for the investigation.

The tea arrived at this point, and after the clatter had subsided Mr. Ogilvie asked her a few questions.

"Was there anyone else on the boat deck during the entire time that you were there?"

"No," said Lady Marsh, "there was no one person there all the time. Mr. Imhoff was there when I went up, but he went away about fifteen minutes later."

"And you say you went up just before three?"

"Yes. While I was there Chet Gordon came up and wandered around and finally asked me to play a game of deck tennis."

There was a laugh, which Mr. Ogilvie stamped out with a sweeping glance.

"At what time was that?" he asked.

"About fifteen minutes after Mr. Imhoff left."

"Did you play with him?"

"No."

"What did he do then?"

"He stood at the rail for a while and then went off."

"Did anyone else come up?"

"Only my daughters," said Lady Marsh. "They came up at about five to four and asked me to come down to tea."

"Did you go dwn with them?"

"No. They went on ahead. I addressed the letters I had written and then followed them down."

Lady Marsh was excused, and Mr. Imhoff was called and asked to relate his activities. He took up much less time. He had gone to the boat deck directly after lunch and dozed there until a little after three, when he had gone to his cabin and written some letters. After that he had gone up to the smoke room with a book.

"What time did you get up to the smoke room?" asked Mr. Ogilvie.

"At about a quarter to four."

He was excused, and I leaned over and asked Robert in a whisper if he knew at what time Mrs. Jennings had been killed.

"They're not sure," he whispered back, "but they think somewhere from half-past three to four."

Mr. Ogilvie caught us whispering and gave us a stern glance, and I felt as though I were back in school.

Celia was called next. She had taken the inevitable nap after lunch and then had gone to the promenade deck for her afternoon walk.

"At what time was that?" asked Mr. Ogilvie.

Celia said self-consciously, "I'm afraid it was pretty late. I was tired, and I slept more than usual."

Mr. Ogilvie passed it over impatiently. "Yes, yes, but what time was it?"

"It was just on twenty after three when I got up on deck."

"For how long did you walk?"

"Ten minutes."

"Did you at any time look in the windows of the drawing room?"

"Yes," said Celia. "Mrs. Jennings was knitting there. I looked in after my walk, and I decided to go in and have a chat with her."

"And did you go?" asked the purser eagerly.

"Yes. I went in and talked with her for ten minutes, then she told me she had an appointment for tea, so I left her. She seemed to want me to go."

"You say you were there for about ten minutes?"

"Just about—yes, because a little later I looked at my watch, and it was a quarter of four."

"Did Mrs. Jennings tell you with whom she had the appointment for tea?"

Celia colored painfully, wrung her hands and gave me an anguished look.

"You will please tell us who it was, Miss Merton," Mr. Ogilvie said sternly. It was quite obvious that she knew.

She gave me one last glance, dropped her eyes to her lap and said faintly, "Carla. Carla Bray."

CHAPTER FORTY

I HAD KNOWN it was coming, of course, but up to the last minute I had hoped that someone else might have had an appointment with Mrs. Jennings before myself.

I sat there while everybody turned and stared at me. Mr. Ogilvie's stare was the worst—there was something ominous about it. I stared back at him, finding nothing to say.

When he spoke his voice was almost mild. "Miss Bray, will you describe your afternoon's activities?"

I described them in detail. He himself, of course, could corroborate a certain amount of it, but when I came to the part about meeting Mrs. Jennings for tea so that she could tell me something about the murders he looked absolutely ashamed for me. I could see him thinking, "Clumsy attempt on the part of Miss Bray to direct suspicion elsewhere."

I was beginning to stumble, in my effort to make it sound as natural as it actually was, when he excused me abruptly and called on Peter Condit.

Peter said tersely, "Have been drinking steadily in my cabin ever since lunch until asked by steward to come up here."

Mr. Ogilvie's stern, Presbyterian forebears appeared briefly in his face before he asked courteously, "What did you do besides drink, Mr. Condit?"

"Tried to sleep and failed, broke a glass, cursed roundly—"

"Is that all you did?"

"Yes."

He could get nothing more out of Peter, so he turned to Chet.

Chet had read on the promenade deck for half an hour after lunch and then had wandered about the decks for a while. He did not know what time it was when he asked Lady Marsh to play deck tennis, but shortly before four he had gone down to wash up for tea.

"You spent an hour and a half just wandering about the decks?" Mr. Ogilvie asked skeptically.

"Certainly," said Chet indignantly.

Mr. Ogilvie looked doubtful, but I knew perfectly well that Chet had spent a large part of the voyage doing just that. If he couldn't find anyone to play deck tennis or shuffleboard with him he'd wander around aimlessly, hardly ever bothering to sit down. As for the book he was reading, he had kept doggedly at it during the entire voyage. He always opened it after lunch, with the double purpose of digesting his enormous meal and getting through a few more pages. Half an hour sounded overlong for him to have been at it, however.

Mr. Ogilvie passed him off and turned his attention to Lucy and Phyllis.

Lucy did the speaking as usual. "We always have a little sleep after lunch, and we did today, as usual. After that we went to the writing room, and Phyllis read a book while I wrote some letters. At about five to four we went up to the boat deck to get Mamma to come down for tea. We came down ahead of her and went to our cabin and washed up, and then as we came up the stairs a steward told us to go to the smoke room."

Mr. Ogilvie said respectfully, "Thank you, Miss Marsh. You, Sir Alfred—"

Sir Alfred must have been sleeping with his eyes open, for he gave a little start and blinked owlishly.

"Er—yes," he said. "Well, I'm afraid I can't help you. I know nothing about it."

"If you could tell us what you did this afternoon?" Mr. Ogilvie suggested patiently.

"Oh—well—lot of rot, really. Doesn't help at all. I slept."

"You slept?"

"Yes, I slept."

"Did you sleep all the time from after lunch until you were called?"

"Good God, man!" said Sir Alfred, suddenly losing patience. "I was lying on my bed. What confounded difference does it make whether I slept or not?"

"I'm sorry to have to trouble you," said Mr. Ogilvie coldly, "but these questions are absolutely necessary. Did you sleep all the time?"

"I removed my boots and collar," said Sir Alfred furiously, "lay down on the bed and opened a book at page 19. I read a few pages, then I blew my nose, read another page and fell asleep. The book was lying on my chest—page 23—when I woke up."

"Sir Alfred," Lady Marsh put in pacifically, "doesn't sleep very well at night." I think she felt that some explanation was due as to why he slept almost continuously during the day.

Mr. Ogilvie drew himself up and swept us with a glance. He looked like a man about to do his duty, however distasteful.

Peter staved off the evil moment by asking suddenly, "What about Mr. Arnold?"

"I was with Mr. Arnold myself practically the entire afternoon," the purser said coldly.

Peter raised his eyebrows. "Then may I inquire into the activities of the two of you for the afternoon?"

Mr. Ogilvie's face flushed a dull red. Robert laughed and said, "Why not? Everyone else has confessed to how long he slept."

He gave a brief account of the afternoon. He mentioned the discussion in his room merely as a talk but said nothing as to its nature. After leaving his cabin they had gone to the purser's office and had continued to talk until ten to four, when Mr. Ogilvie had announced that he simply must catch up on some of his regular work, and Robert had gone up to the smoke room, where I found him.

"So now, who did it?" asked Peter carelessly. He was pretty drunk.

The Marsh girls giggled and were hushed into frozen silence by a look from their mother.

Robert said suddenly, "Lucy, were you sitting in the writing room in such a position that you had command of the drawing-room door? I know it can be seen from certain parts of the writing room."

Lucy shook her head. "I had my back to it."

"How about Phyllis?"

Phyllis said shyly, "Yes, I was facing the door—it was open—and I looked up from my reading now and then."

"Did you see anyone enter the drawing room?"

"Well—Celia. And Carla."

"What time?" asked Mr. Ogilvie eagerly.

Phyllis shook her head unhappily. "I don't know," she said lamely.

Mr. Ogilvie sighed and asked resignedly, "Who went in first?"

"Celia."

I twisted my hands together nervously. She had not seen me go in the first time then, as I had supposed, but only the second time, when I discovered the murder.

"How long did Miss Bray stay there?" Ogilvie asked.

"I don't know," said Phyllis. "I didn't see her come out."

"But I did come out," I said anxiously.

"By the same door?" Mr. Ogilvie pounced.

"Yes."

He turned to Phyllis. "But you did not see her come out?"

"No—but we left right after that to go up and get Mamma."

"Oh yes. And that was at about five to four?"

"Yes."

"How long before that did Miss Bray enter the drawing room?"

Phyllis went into a brown study and finally brought forth, "I don't know, exactly. Just a few minutes, I imagine."

"It couldn't have been long," I put in, "as I went in there almost exactly at five of four—and they went up to get Lady Marsh at five of four also."

Mr. Ogilvie withered me with a look and returned to Phyllis.

"When you went out of the writing room you did not encounter Miss Bray leaving the drawing room?"

Lucy and Phyllis said, "No," in unison.

"But then," Lucy mused, "Phyllis half sleeps when she reads, like Father, so she might have been dozing when Carla came out."

For once Phyllis showed some spunk. "I was not dozing," she said angrily. "I was reading, and I didn't sleep a wink."

Lucy looked mildly shocked. "I don't see how you can tell such fibs, Phyl—you know very well you dozed several times this afternoon. Why, once when I spoke to you, you didn't answer, so I looked around at you, and there you were, sleeping soundly."

"It's you who are telling lies!" Phyllis cried hotly and got up and left the room.

We all watched her go, gaping a bit. We'd never seen the Marsh girls quarreling before.

Lady Marsh clicked her tongue. "You know she doesn't like one to notice it, Lucy, when she falls asleep over a book. Why did you ruffle her about it?"

Lucy shrugged. "Well, she needn't have been so ill-natured about it. After all, there is nothing wrong with sleeping while you read."

"Nothing at all," said Peter gravely. "It saves you from getting bored."

Mr. Ogilvie cleared his throat peremptorily, and we all looked at him.

"Miss Bray, didn't you enter the drawing room somewhat earlier than five to four?"

"No," I said emphatically, "I did not—and my watch is right. I did not want to annoy her by coming too early."

"Why did you look in the window?"

"I was getting impatient. The time seemed to go so slowly—I thought I'd see if she looked ready to receive me or not."

He looked hard at me. "The drawing room is public, Miss Bray; Mrs. Jennings could hardly have resented it had you sat in there to await your tea."

I looked at him helplessly and couldn't say a word. How could I explain that Mrs. Jennings did consider that room as hers and might have been so annoyed, had I arrived too early, as to refuse to tell what she had hinted she could?

There was a long silence which Mr. Ogilvie finally broke by saying solemnly, "Miss Bray, I'm sorry, but I shall have to keep you locked in your cabin until we get in."

CHAPTER FORTY-ONE

I WAS MAINLY CONSCIOUS of a silly desire to cry. It had been all right to joke about being put into irons, but now that it had actually happened I felt dazed and horrified. Why, I was being arrested for murder—I, Carla Bray.

There was a sort of general gasp, and everybody turned and looked at me. Robert stood up. He looked angry, but his voice was unusually gentle when he spoke. "Come on, Carla, let's go down. It's only until tomorrow, you know. Mr. Ogilvie is making a mistake."

He took my arm, and Mr. Ogilvie muttered something and fell in with us on my other side. I stopped wanting to cry at that point and felt a hysterical desire to laugh instead. I said idiotically, "You should each have a gun and walk one in front and one behind me."

Robert chuckled, and Mr. Ogilvie looked uncomfortable and offended.

When we got to my cabin Robert wanted to be locked in with me—he said he had to talk to me. Mr. Ogilvie objected on the grounds that it was highly irregular and that the captain would not like it. Robert gave in with a shrug, and Mr. Ogilvie carefully locked me in by myself.

I sat down on the bed, and I think I must have sat there for an hour, miserably doing nothing. Then the connecting door opened, and Robert came through from his own room.

"Nice day, isn't it?" he said.

I just looked at him.

"Ogilvie made quite a point of padlocking you off from the corridor, but my room and the connecting door are open. He'll never get a job with the G-men."

"Funny, aren't you?" I said disgustedly.

"I have to get your attention somehow. I want to talk to you."

"What about? It's all quite simple. Uncle Henry will get me a lawyer, and after I'm acquitted I'll live in disgrace for the rest of my life."

He actually laughed. "What do you care? Your grandchildren will love it."

"All very comical," I said bitterly. "Why don't you go up and laugh over it with Lucy and Phyllis?"

He dropped the banter from his voice and said quietly, "Why do you insist in throwing my attentions back in my face?"

"What attentions?" I asked shortly.

He got up abruptly and took a turn about the room. When he faced me again he was smiling faintly. "Haven't you noticed my attentions?"

"No," I said, "come to think of it, I really haven't. If what you gave me were attentions I'd like to know what's been going on between you and the Marsh girls."

He stared down at me. "Surely you're not jealous of poor Lucy?"

I turned away from him. If I was the same woman Mr. Ogilvie had wanted to lock up before tea, then I must be the woman with whom Robert was in love.

I decided to ask him if Mr. Ogilvie had suspected me all the afternoon, but when I opened my mouth I heard myself ask, "Are you in love with me?"

"Yes."

"Am I the same woman you were in love with before tea?"

He went over to the window, leaned his arms on the sill and stared out without answering.

"Because if I'm the same one you've been in love with all along," I went on, "I've seen mighty little of you."

He came back and faced me again. "I know that but I didn't want you to tire of me."

He leaned over and pulled me to my feet and, holding my hands behind me, looked down into my face. "Darling, I do love you—can't you tell?" He laughed a little. "Isn't there supposed to be something called woman's intuition that should have told you I love you?"

"Yes," I said flatly, "there certainly is a thing called woman's intuition. Whenever you want a man to be in love with you, your woman's intuition tells you he is. It gets to be quite embarrassing at times."

"What about this time?"

"I didn't consult it. I merely looked into my head, and it shook itself sadly and said no."

"Sadly?" he asked, smiling down at me.

I turned my head away. "Oh—give me a cigarette."

He released me abruptly and supplied me in silence, and we both sat down again.

"Do we start all over again?" I asked after a while.

"I don't know," he said doubtfully. "I was getting worked up to proposing to you, but I'm beginning to think I'd better write you a letter."

"Perhaps you had. I don't see you except at odd intervals, like this."

"But I'm going to explain all that."

"Then you want me to take you on approval?"

"And you, perhaps," he said ominously, "want me to box your ears?"

"Explain all," I said airily.

"Well, stop interrupting me. I fell in love with you right at the start."

"Liar."

"But you were getting plenty of attention from the men, and Lucy and Phyllis were not. Now I know that business brings business, so I figured that if I gave Lucy and Phyllis a rush it might bring some of the other men around and leave you alone for me."

"Very fishy," I observed.

"Well, I'm always sorry for girls like that— Mother intent on making belles out of them—and it usually works the other way."

"Very noble."

"Be quiet," he said, "or I *will* box your ears. To go on—I realized that the attractive women were getting killed off, and I wanted to give people the impression that you were not attractive."

I laughed and said, "Don't be silly."

He ignored that and cleared his throat. "I want you to help me tonight," he said. "You've got to help me. I'm sure I can clear this up—and if I do your uncle won't have to bother about a lawyer, and Ogilvie will look a fool. You must help me, for your own sake. I have a plan."

I folded my handkerchief carefully, shook it out again and crumpled it into a ball. "But—can't you tell me more about it?" I asked uncertainly.

"Not now—I can't. I have to go anyway. After I've kissed you, that is."

"I don't think I'll let you kiss me," I said feebly.

He got up and came towards me purposefully. "I'll toss a coin: heads I do and tails I don't."

"All right," I said with dignity.

It came out heads.

After a little while he said, "I'm going up now to Lady Marsh and tell her that I was going to marry one of her daughters, but now I have to marry you because of the scandal about you having slept in my cabin. I shall ask her to see to the wedding arrangements, and she can get Sir Alfred for best man—provided he can manage to stay awake that long. The captain will marry us, and the wedding is to be tonight."

"We'll let Mr. Ogilvie be master of ceremonies," I added.

"Now I'll have to go," he said regretfully. "I'm going to sit with Celia and buy her a bottle of champagne. Don't forget to lock the door after me."

"Oh, I'll be safe," I said, "but Celia had better watch her step."

CHAPTER FORTY-TWO

A STEWARD CAME IN after a while and took my order for dinner. It was painfully embarrassing to have the man unlock the door, hand in the menu, then carefully lock up again after he had received my order.

When he had gone I stretched out on my bed and tried to think things over. I could not get my thoughts into line though. Things seemed to be whirling around in my head, and all I knew was that I was extraordinarily happy—and a little frightened.

My dinner came in after a while, and when I had finished it I settled down and tried to read. But I could not concentrate. My thoughts be-

came confused again. I found myself wondering when Robert was coming back.

I laughed a little and glanced nervously over my shoulder at the
window—but there were no leering ghosts peering in—it was quite blank.

There was a knock on the door. I had heard no approaching footsteps, and I started and swung my eyes uneasily around. I called, "Yes?"
in a rather quavering voice—but it was only the steward come for the
dinner things.

I returned to my chair and began to wonder why Robert was staying
away from me when he was supposed to be protecting me from some
sort of danger. I wondered what his plan had been, and I determined to
make him explain it to me clearly when he came back.

There was another knock on the door, and I felt the prickle of hair
on my scalp. I gripped the arms of my chair and called out, "Yes?" in an
unnaturally loud voice.

It was Lady Marsh. She said shrilly, through the door, "How are you,
my dear?"

"As well as could be expected," I answered flippantly.

"My dear, it's a shame. Mr. Ogilvie has made a terrible mistake, I'm
sure."

"Yes," I said, wishing she would go away.

"Do you know where Robert Arnold is? We're looking for a fourth."

I laughed to myself. The old hellcat was trying to find out if he was
with me.

"No, I don't," I said shortly.

She clicked her tongue. "We can't seem to get anyone. Peter is indisposed, Mr. Imhoff doesn't play, and the girls are doing some last-
minute laundry work. And Alfred and Celia and I are dying to play."

I made no reply, so she said, "Good-by for the present—I'll come
back later, and we'll have another little chat."

I lay down on the bed again and made another attempt to read my
book—but it was no use. I could not follow the story, and I presently put
it aside and simply stared at the ceiling and listened to the ship's movements.

My thoughts drifted uneasily to Sally, and I found myself getting
restless. Suppose she was wandering around the room at this very minute,
putting fingerprints onto things!

I told myself not to be a fool, and I think I dozed for a while. I came
awake with a start to the sound of some sort of movement in Robert's
room.

I got up quickly and called out, but it was Mr. Ogilvie who answered.

"He seems to have disappeared, Miss Bray. I wanted to talk with him, but I couldn't find him, so I thought I'd look in his cabin. He's not here though."

I said, "Oh," rather flatly and was glad I hadn't gone through the door and so showed him that it was not locked.

An idea occurred to me, and I called out, "Mr. Ogilvie—have you found the object that was used to hit Mrs. Jennings on the head?"

"No," he said briefly.

"Well, in all fairness to me I'd like you to find it. I suppose you had my cabin searched while we were being questioned?"

"Yes."

"You didn't find anything here?"

"Yes, we did," he said unexpectedly. "We found a bloodstained hand-kerchief belonging to Mrs. Jennings."

"What!"

He did not answer, and I heard him go out.

I sat back on the bed, and the whole thing started whirling through my head again.

Irrelevantly I wondered why Lady Marsh had chatted so sweetly after cutting me dead only a few hours before and decided that it was simply vulgar curiosity. She wanted to know how I was feeling and whether Robert was with me.

And where was Robert? He had said he had a plan and that I was to help him—but I was still completely in the dark as to what it was about. I was conscious of a vague, uneasy doubt about him.

A gentle tap on the door at this point turned out to be Celia.

"I wanted to tell you that I think Ogilvie's crazy," she said. "Anybody ought to know that you couldn't have had anything to do with it."

I thanked her rather wearily.

"I think one of the crew has gone insane. I've heard that that does happen sometimes. You know—the work they have to do," she added vaguely.

"Well—I don't know," I said doubtfully, thinking of a member of the crew arrayed in my dressing robe. "How did the captain's dinner go off?"

"It didn't," said Celia. "Neither the captain nor the decorations appeared."

"Oh. Well, what happened to Lady Marsh's party?"

"Was she going to have a party?"

"Yes, indeed," I said. "She was gathering all the men into the fold, and you and I were to be left out."

Celia laughed. "Then it was a flop. There were no men at her table—unless you want to call Sir Alfred a man. I heard that Mr. Condit was drunk, and I think he stayed in his cabin. Mr. Arnold came to my table for some reason, and Chet ate with Dr. Barton as usual."

I asked her about the champagne, and she said that Chet had wandered over and drunk most of it.

"Tell me," she said suddenly, "did Lady Marsh come down to chat with you?"

"Yes, she did," I said, laughing a little. "It was rather hard on her, too, because she's not speaking to me."

"Why?" asked Celia curiously.

"Moral grounds. Sleeping too close to Robert without a door between."

She laughed, and we chatted for a while longer; then she went off.

I started to think about Peter. He had not mentioned his talks with us, about his having been married to Kay, but it was natural enough, I decided. He had been mixed up with both Kay and Sally, to a certain extent—and I thought, aggrievedly, that he looked quite as guilty as I did. No wonder he was lying drunk in his cabin. I moved restlessly and wished that I was in a drunken stupor too.

I felt sure that Mrs. Jennings had been murdered to keep her from telling me anything. The murderer must have heard us when she promised to tell me what she knew at tea.

Whoever it was must have been pretty badly frightened, for the murder—in broad daylight and in full view of several windows—had been a thoroughly daring piece of work.

My mind went back to Peter and the questioning in the smoke room. Peter had lied. He had told Mr. Ogilvie that he had gone straight to his cabin after lunch, and he had been up in the smoke room, having coffee and liqueurs with Lucy and later talking to Robert and me.

Celia had left Mrs. Jennings at about twenty minutes to four, and I had gone in at five to four; and somebody had murdered her brutally in that fifteen minutes. Phyllis had not seen anyone else enter the room, but of course the murderer might have come through the door on the other side. I became so confused that I gave up thinking: about it and decided that I'd better get out my favorite dress, because if they freed me later on I intended to go straight upstairs and get a bottle of champagne.

I looked idly through the wardrobe and, coming to my nicest evening gown, fingered it and wondered whether it would be appropriate for champagne drinking. I started to lift it out and discovered that part of the skirt was held taut. I frowned and, stooping down to see what was catching it, found the small iron that Aunt Edna had given me to press my dresses. I had never used it. I had told her that I wouldn't, and I felt a spasm of annoyance that the thing should be knocking about in my wardrobe, injuring my favorite dress.

I picked it up—and was enveloped in a wave of sick horror. The point and bottom of the thing were stained with blood.

CHAPTER FORTY-THREE

I STARED AT THE THING and was conscious of an intense longing to throw it out into the sea. I think I should have done just that if my porthole had given on to the water, but I was pretty sure that I could never throw it the width of the deck and high enough to go over the rail.

It had my fingerprints on it now too. I wondered why they had not found it when they discovered the bloodstained handkerchief. I had an impulse to wash the thing carefully and put it away but was deterred by a vague fear that they had left it as a trap—were, perhaps, just waiting to see what I would do with it.

I hesitated, confused and upset. I felt that I had no right to destroy evidence, but it seemed like hanging myself to show it to Mr. Ogilvie.

I decided at last to ask Robert about it and rang the bell for the steward. It was about ten minutes before he knocked on the door, and I asked him to find Robert at once and tell him I wanted to speak to him.

The steward promised to do so and went away. I found that I still held the iron in my hand, and I put it gingerly back where I had found it, pushing my dresses carefully to one side.

I sat down to wait then—and I waited nearly an hour. Finally, yielding to impatience and suspense, I rang again. After an interval the steward came and said through the door, "I'm very sorry, miss, but Mr. Arnold can't be found anywhere. Mr. Ogilvie has been looking for him for some time—and he's not on the decks or in the lounges. Mr. Ogilvie is having the cabins searched."

My heart turned over, and I twisted cold, clammy hands together futilely. I sank into the armchair and gave myself over to agonizing mental pictures of Robert lying dead in one of the empty cabins.

I couldn't stand it at last. I got up and rang the bell again. When the steward came I could tell by his voice that he was getting pretty annoyed about it.

I told him to get Mr. Ogilvie—that I had found some important evidence.

He said, "Yes, miss," in a surprised voice. I suppose he thought it funny that the accused should not only find further evidence, but should decide to show it as well.

It was almost twenty minutes before Mr. Ogilvie came. He knocked, and I called, "Come in," knowing that he had the key.

He came in looking very cross. "What is it, Miss Bray? I'm very busy just now."

"Have you found Robert yet?" I asked abruptly.

He froze visibly and said, "Is that all you wanted me for?"

"No, no," I said impatiently. "I really have something important to show you—but you must tell me, first, if you have found him."

He shook his head. "Not yet. We're looking through the cabins now."

I turned away, trying to blink back the tears.

"What is it you wanted to show me?" he asked, a shade less austerely.

I opened the wardrobe and indifferently indicated the iron. "Your searcher wasn't particularly good in this room."

He looked at it for a moment and then bent down and picked it up. I wanted to laugh. He'd spoiled my fingerprints, at any rate.

He examined the thing for a while and stared thoughtfully at the dried blood. Then he looked at me queerly.

"I suppose you're surprised at my having showed it to you," I suggested.

"A little."

"Somebody deliberately planted it there," I said flatly.

He shrugged and turned towards the door, the iron still in his hand.

"Wait a minute," I begged. "Please tell me more about Robert. Why have you started a search for him—since I'm safely locked up?"

He hesitated, with his hand on the door, and his shoulders seemed to droop a little. "I don't know—the thing has got me jumpy. I could not find him when I wanted to talk to him, so I immediately imagined that something must have happened to him. I'm doing the best I can, but I'll be glad when I can hand it over, tomorrow, to someone more capable."

I felt that the mighty had fallen a bit, and I was glad that he did not seem absolutely sure of my guilt. But I was terribly frightened and nervous about Robert.

"Oh, please let me know when you find him," I begged.

"I will," said Mr. Ogilvie and went out. I heard him lock the door and walk off with a slightly lagging step.

I had nothing to do then—nothing but to sit and worry about Robert. I paced the floor, sat down, got up to look out of the window, paced the floor again and worried without ceasing. I don't think I have ever spent a more painful evening.

After what seemed an eternity I looked at the clock and found that it was just twelve, but I could not face going to bed. At twelve-fifteen I felt that I was heading for desperation and hysterics when there was a knock on the door.

It was Peter, still, apparently, very drunk. "Are you locked in?" he asked thickly.

"Yes."

"They're a bunch of dirty guys," he said indignantly. "Of all the highly suspicious people they could have locked up, they go and pick on a fine pal like you."

I couldn't help laughing. Peter had certainly lost his poise this time.

"As a matter of fact," he continued, "I wanted a bit of advice from you. Which would be better—a witty gentleman, frayed at the cuff and often thirsty, but free, or the same witty gentleman, smartly turned out, never thirsty, paying his respects to his fine connections—and walking out on the little woman every evening that he can damn well get away?"

"It's a real stinker, Peter," I told him. "Maybe you'd better marry her. If you break her heart, at least she'll enjoy telling people that she's lived. And as far as you're concerned—"

"As far as I'm concerned," he took me up, "it may not matter. One may quite well be a dead gentleman, no longer witty and no longer thirsty—and without cuffs of any sort."

"I think you'd better go to bed."

"That's what she will be saying," he murmured dispiritedly. " 'I don't think you'd better drink any more, dear. Don't you think we'd better go, dear? Darling, do come and look at Junior—he's so sweet when he says his prayers.' "

He copied Lucy's voice so perfectly that I laughed hysterically. "Peter, do shut up. Somebody will hear you."

"Christmas," said Peter hollowly. "Christmas will be a home day. Papa, Mamma, Aunt Annie." He lurched against the door with a dull thud. "Aunt Annie will give me a penwiper, and I will give Aunt Annie a pincushion—selected and wrapped, of course, by my dear wife—who will be back-patted and cooed over for having gone to so much trouble in her condition."

I laughed helplessly and told him again to go to bed.

"Perhaps you're right," he sighed. "And mark you, I shall lock the door, because in spite of everything I should prefer to be Mr. Lucy Marsh than a name on a tombstone. Good night, my friend—your only fault is your poverty."

I heard his uncertain departure and shook my head over him.

He had evidently got to the great decision point, and it had got him stewed to the eyebrows.

I resumed my pacing, and when that grew intolerable I rang the hell again. The steward did not come, and though I rang several times there was no response.

I broke into tears—and at that moment I heard someone enter Robert's room.

I cried nervously, "Robert, is that you?"

There was no answer, and I heard footsteps cross the room to my door. I stood by the armchair, my hand clutching its back and my nerves quivering.

That connecting door was not locked, and anybody—anything— could get in to me.

I took a step forward, my hand stretched to fasten the lock, but it was too late.

I stared, speechless, as the knob turned and the door swung slowly inwards.

CHAPTER FORTY-FOUR

I WATCHED THE DOOR, fascinated, unable to move, and with one small portion of my brain wondering how I could protect myself against what was coming in.

The door finally swung wide enough to reveal Robert, finger held at his lips for silence.

I gave a little gasp of surprise and infinite relief, and he came in and softly closed the door and then listened at it for a moment.

"What on earth is it?" I whispered, mopping at my wet eyes and feeling that I'd scream if he did not say something.

He stretched out an arm and switched off the light and then made his way noiselessly to me in the darkness. I felt the relaxing of my nerves and a sense of peace as he put his arms around me.

He touched my face gently with his fingers, and I could see him shake his head. "You're the cryingest woman I ever met," he said softly. "You'll have to pull yourself together. We're going to have a visitor."

"Robert Arnold, where have you been?" I whispered fiercely.

"I'll tell you afterwards " He laughed silently. "I've been damned uncomfortable. Now listen, dear. I want you to get into bed and lie quietly, as though you were asleep. I'm expecting the murderer."

"The—the murderer . . . ?" I faltered.

"Yes—to finish you off. I'm going to get some real evidence this time."

"But—does Mr. Ogilvie know where you are? He's been searching all over the place."

"Yes, I know. I've called him and his bloodhounds off."

"But, Robert—where have you been?"

He kissed me and murmured, "Hush, darling. Get into bed—and be as quiet as you can."

He guided me through the darkness to the bed, but I clung desperately to his arm.

"Robert, I—I'll die of fright if that horrible thing comes anywhere near me."

He took my shoulders and gave me a little shake, and I knew he was smiling. "You've got to learn to trust the old man. I'll be here with you all the time."

"Can't we fix a pillow in the bed?" I suggested feebly.

"Not good enough. Come on—in you go. And don't worry or be nervous. I'll take care of you."

"Suppose you fall asleep?"

He lifted me without a word and laid me down on the bed. He arranged the quilt over me and then made his way quietly to a corner opposite the door leading to his room. I could just see him standing there in the dim light.

I settled down to wait, nervous and restless, but forcing myself to be still. I was far from comfortable. I was too hot, for one thing, as I had not undressed and Robert had pulled the quilt up to my chin. I was supposed to be asleep, so that I could not move much, and my body was stiff and aching in five minutes.

I could see the square of window by just opening my eyes, and I could make out the door leading to Robert's cabin, but as time went on I realized that I could no longer see Robert. I could not hear him, either, and I began to wonder uneasily if he were still there.

Then I began to think I heard someone moving outside on the deck, but after straining my ears for some time I decided that I had been mistaken.

I started to concentrate on any noise that seemed to come from Robert's room, for that was evidently the direction from which Robert expected our visitor. At first I kept thinking that someone was coming in—I was sure I could hear creaks and footfalls—but they always turned out to be false alarms. After a time I got to recognize some of the creaks as coming regularly, and the other sounds, I knew, were just the usual ship's noises. I wished fretfully that they were not so loud, as I wanted to be sure and hear any alien noise at once.

Suddenly there was a new sound—a short, sharp tap—and it seemed to come from where Robert was. It was not very loud but quite distinct—certainly not one of the ship's noises.

I stood it for a while, and then I raised my head in alarm. "Robert!"

"Quiet!" came his reply instantly.

I lay back again, trying to relax. The tapping had ceased.

For a while nothing happened, and then the sharp, irritating little sound started up again. It was no louder, and it still seemed to come from where Robert was standing. It seemed to make the suspense and waiting infinitely harder. I knew that Robert must hear it, too, and I wondered anxiously why he did not do something about it.

I tried to forget it and to think about Robert instead. I was sure I loved him and I was sure that he loved me too. Aunt Edna and Uncle Henry, I thought, would probably disapprove when they heard about it—they'd say I hardly knew the man. Well, that was true enough, of course. I didn't know much about him—except that he seemed to have rather unconventional ideas! In fact, who and what was he? Although I could see it coming and tried valiantly to fight it off the idea that perhaps he was the murderer slid into my mind and sat there, jeering at me.

I shivered. Hadn't Mrs. Jennings suspected him early on? I tried a mental laugh at the thought, but the laugh was feeble.

I lay quite still, trying not to tremble, and listened intently. And then I heard him take a step towards me.

Panic brought the sweat out on my forehead, and I heard myself gasp. He was coming now to finish me off!

I gripped the side of my berth and felt a scream strangle in my throat. Then I realized that he had stopped—that he had taken only one step. I swallowed my panic and wondered feverishly why I had been such a gullible fool. Here I lay in my bed, a murderer loose on the ship, and I allowed a man I hardly knew to stay in the cabin with me!

The tapping had stopped again, but there was some other, faint noise. Panic drenched me again as I thought that he was probably creeping over the floor towards me.

I was diverted by the window. A deeper shadow had fallen across it, and, straining my eyes fearfully, I could see that someone was looking in. I lay deadly still and watched. I could make out the side of a head, and I thought I could see one eye, but the light was so dim that nothing was clear.

The thing disappeared suddenly, and I continued to stare at the blank space. I wondered almost coldly, now, whether Robert was still crawling across the floor to me.

I forced my eyes from the window and looked at the floor, but there did not seem to be any dark, creeping shape there.

I cautiously stretched my aching body, and at that instant I distinctly heard Robert's door click and soft footsteps crossing his room.

I became still and alert, my eyes fixed on the connecting door. I heard the click of the handle, and it swung slowly inwards. I remember thinking quite coolly, "This is the murderer coming to finish me off."

The door opened very slowly, and for a while nothing appeared. Then quite silently a dim shape slipped through. I could not tell who or even what it was. It came straight towards me, and it seemed to grow enormously in proportion as it got closer. It reached the bed at last and seemed to tower blackly above me—and then I noticed that a rope dangled from its hand.

It leaned over me, and wild terror rose into my throat. I tried to call to Robert, and the only sound that came was a low whimper.

Light suddenly flooded the room, and the figure straightened jerkily.

I struggled frantically out of the bed and pressed against the wall.

Robert said quietly, "I'm afraid it's all over, Phyllis."

I flung up my head and stared at her as Mr. Ogilvie unlocked the door to the corridor and stepped into the room.

Phyllis wore a crepe nightgown and a plain cotton dressing gown. Her eyes were unrecognizable. She backed away slowly and spoke once, in a high, harsh voice.

"Yes, I killed them, because they got in my way. I'm sorry I didn't get her." She gestured at me.

She turned suddenly and flew through the connecting door into Robert's room.

The two men ran after her, and after a moment of confusion I went out into the corridor through the door that Mr. Ogilvie had just unlocked. Through the window I caught a glimpse of Phyllis running along the deck, and I hurried out there.

She was far along towards the end of the ship by then, her gown and robe flying out behind her. The men were gaining on her, and I struggled after them, breathing in long gasps.

I saw her mount the rail at the stern and hover there for a moment—then she went over, glimmering in the darkness like some great bird. There was a faint splash and a flicker of foam.

I felt my body sag against the rail, shaking hands pressed against my horrified eyes.

CHAPTER FORTY-FIVE

ROBERT CAME TO ME, and we stood there for a while as the white patch that was Phyllis shrank to a speck and finally disappeared.

Mr. Ogilvie had run off, shouting. Presently I noticed that the ship had stopped and that they were getting out some of the lifeboats.

Lights had sprung up in the smoke room, and Robert took me there and managed to get a glass of brandy for me.

I don't know how long they looked for Phyllis, but they never found her. I was conscious of Lucy, white-faced and tearful, and Sir Alfred, his hands shaking oddly, saying that Phyllis could not swim a stroke. Lady Marsh did not appear, and someone said that she was having violent hysterics in her cabin.

I think it was about three o'clock when the ship started up again, and shortly after that Robert, Mr. Ogilvie, the captain and I assembled in the captain's sitting room. A steward had brought coffee and sandwiches, and as we ate Robert reconstructed the whole story for us.

"I noticed Phyllis particularly," he said, "the first time I saw her talking privately to Chet. They were on the boat deck, and they did not know that I was there.

"Chet was leaning on the rail, his attitude unmistakably negligent and indifferent, but I was surprised to see that Phyllis was displaying a sort of forced and jerky animation. She was flirting—as well as she knew how—and it interested me, because she had always seemed much too timid and prim for anything of the sort. Lucy was always trying it on, of course, but I had vaguely classed Phyllis as the sort to sit and wait for the right man to come along—and if he didn't it was God's will, etc. I decided that I had been wrong about her, that she was trying to take matters into her own hands, no matter how awkwardly.

"I watched her—at that time merely amused at the difference between her and Lucy. Lucy was obviously doing the best she could for herself. Phyllis, timid and rather stupid on the surface, was working more efficiently towards her own ends, behind people's backs.

"I made it a point to take a walk with Phyllis, alone on the deck one night. I gave her every opportunity but she made no advance whatever. I did a little advancing myself, but she retreated primly and pretended not to notice and she gave me an odd look. I saw, suddenly, that she fully understood what I was up to, and it came as a shock to me that the girl was intelligent—much more so than Lucy.

"I continued to watch her, and several times I heard her make distinctly nasty little remarks about one or other of the attractive women on the boat, and she never missed an opportunity when it was Sally who was being discussed, although Sally was already dead. She always covered up by apparently becoming painfully embarrassed and pretending she had not meant it that way. She did not spare Lucy, either, but Lucy was never sharp enough to see the sting—she placidly accepted the remarks as awkward compliments.

"I discovered that Lady Marsh had determined to marry Lucy off, but she was not wasting any effort on Phyllis, and I overheard her say to Mrs. Jennings that Phyllis was really a home girl and would be a dear, sweet comfort to her parents when they were old.

"She and Sir Alfred were quite unconscious of the fact that Phyllis was a powerful influence in their family affairs—was, in fact, directly responsible for the trip they were taking. Lady Marsh put it this way: 'Phyllis really gave me the idea for this trip, although, of course, she never dreamed of it. She had been to a travel agency with one of her little friends, who was taking a trip to Sydney, and she picked up a few circulars at random. They contained all the information about this very trip we are taking. I suppose it must have been fate.'

"I could have told her that it was Phyllis and not fate, but she probably would not have believed me.

"She had looked over the circulars with interest but had thought she really could not be spared from New Zealand, since she was very active in women's affairs. Then a remark from Phyllis, to the effect that it was a pity an attractive girl like Lucy could not get out and meet more men, so that she might make a brilliant match, served to change Lady Marsh's mind.

"She said to me, 'It was sweet of little Phyllis to think of it, and it is true that Lucy does not care for any of the boys she knows at home.'

"It was clear that Lucy was not getting on, at home, as her mother had hoped—and so the trip followed.

"I discovered that Phyllis was both vain and conceited, although no one seemed to realize it. There was Lucy's remark, 'Oh, Phyllis spends an hour on her hair every morning'; and Lady Marsh, sewing on one of Phyllis' dresses, explained, 'The child can't sew at all. I have to do all her things. Just now she's sure her dresses are an inch too long, and the poor darling is so sensitive. So I'm humoring her and taking them up.'

"Later I ran across Sir Alfred telling three riddles to Lucy, Phyllis and Chet. A steward had just told them to him and caught him on every one, and he was anxious to catch someone else. He told the first one, and while Lucy and Chet looked vaguely puzzled Phyllis gave the correct answer in a shy, apologetic little voice. Lucy and Chet immediately assured Sir Alfred that that was just what they had been going to say. Exactly the same thing happened with the second riddle. But when it came to the third—which was easier than the first two—Phyllis seemed to be stumped. She was still concentrating with a frown when Chet spoke up in a loud voice, and Lucy chimed in with the answer.

"I watched Phyllis, and for an instant her face showed complete dismay, then she collected herself and put on a weak smile. She muttered an excuse that the others did not hear and hurried out onto the deck. I followed her and saw that she was almost running towards the stern of the ship. When I caught up with her she was leaning on the rail, staring out to sea with a look of black anger on her face. As soon as she saw me, of course, her expression changed, and she made some inane remark about the beauty of the water.

"I had a series of talks with Chet, during which I learned that he had had a letter of introduction to the Marshes from a friend of his father's, and he had presented himself as soon as the Marshes embarked at New Zealand.

"He had tried to get off with Sally as soon as they left Sydney, but Sally wasn't having any, and after the Marshes came on board he gave Phyllis a little attention. He had been sitting with Phyllis in the smoke room, a couple of days after New Zealand, when Sally had descended on them and after an interval of gay chatter had calmly asked Chet to come out and walk the deck with her. Chet had jumped at it, of course, and, as far as I can gather, had not bothered with Phyllis again until two days before Tahiti.

"At that time Sally told Chet that she could not go ashore with him at Tahiti, as she expected to go with Peter. Chet went off in a huff and wandered the decks for a while. He ran across Phyllis and after playing six games of deck tennis with her suddenly asked her to go ashore with him at Tahiti. She accepted at once.

"The next night Sally came to Chet and without any explanation said that she had decided to go ashore with him after all. He wanted so desperately to go with her that he merely said, 'Thanks awfully,' and then went to Phyllis with some awkward excuse that 'owing to unforeseen circumstances, etc.' Chet said to me that Phyllis had not cared at all, but I knew he was wrong.

"Later, at Tahiti, while Sally and Chet were doing the sights they ran into the Marsh family, and after an exchange of greetings Sally said to Lady Marsh, 'I see you still have your girls by your side.'

"Lady Marsh replied quickly, 'Oh yes, indeed. That's where they belong until they have their proper debut in London.'

"Chet said that Sally had laughed heartily at the incident once they were alone, and he was inclined to chuckle about it himself. But I knew that the malice in Sally's remark would have been fully appreciated by Phyllis.

"So far, so good. I had actually got a motive for the murder of Sally. But it did not seem strong enough, nor was I satisfied that a girl could actually have done the thing. It seemed to me it would have taken a man—and a fairly strong one—to have got Sally into that position—and with the cord from her own dressing gown around her neck.

"Then I made two discoveries, the same day, that cleared up both points.

"I had noticed Phyllis with a small blue leather book, which I took to be diary, since she wrote busily in it from time to time. The covers were bound with a clasp and lock, and she never put it aside without carefully locking it. There did not seem a chance of getting a look at it, but one day I was lucky. She had the book at a desk in the writing room and was busy writing in it. I had just stepped in, and she had not noticed me. Lady Marsh called from outside the window, and Phyllis looked up with a frown but made no answer. Lady Marsh called again, and Phyllis stood up impatiently. She clutched at the book, but it fell to the floor, half open. She kept her foot close to it but did not pick it up as she turned to speak to her mother through the window.

"I stepped up quietly, picked up the book and had one glance at the open page before I handed it back to Phyllis as she turned. It was all done so quickly that I think she was sure I had not seen anything, for she seemed quite untroubled.

"As a matter of fact, I had seen only a part of one sentence—but it was highly significant. She had written, '. . . and I will marry Chet, so Carla must go.'

"I went straight down to the cabin where Sally had been murdered, then, convinced that there must be something that led to Phyllis, and I found it.

"I examined the pipe around which the bathrobe cord had been tied. It was covered with some sort of asbestos material, and there was a deep indentation where the cord had been—but right beside it I noticed a much thinner and sharper indentation, and immediately I felt that I understood. I had in my pocket a small piece of thick, stout cord that I had picked off the floor beneath her when we first discovered Sally. It had been cut at each end and was about an inch long. I went straight to Phyllis' cabin and after a brief search found a ball of the same cord—it was identical with the piece I had and was unusual in its strength and thickness.

"While I was there I made a thorough search for the blue diary, but I did not find it then and have not since. I think she must have thrown it overboard."

Robert paused at that point, took a long breath, which he certainly needed, and lighted a cigarette. He looked hopefully at the captain and said, "May I have a drink?"

"Certainly, certainly," said the captain hospitably and poured him a glass of water.

Robert looked at it, sighed, said, "Oh well," and drank it down.

CHAPTER FORTY-SIX

THE CAPTAIN SETTLED himself in his chair again and poured a cup of black coffee. He drank it down and asked curiously, "Do you know anything of how she committed the murders, Mr. Arnold?"

"Yes. Mr. Ogilvie and I have collected bits and pieces of evidence, and I think I have it pretty well put together. Some of it is guesswork, but it must be pretty close to the truth.

"The day you were in at Tahiti Lucy and Phyllis had gone ashore with their parents, since all the available men were escorting the other girls.

"When I came into the smoke room in the evening the two of them were sitting there alone, and I talked to them for a while. Sally, Kay and Chet appeared shortly afterwards, and they came straight over and sat with us, crowding in such a way that Lucy and Phyllis were pushed out a little. Phyllis went off after a while but hovered in and out of the smoke room and watched us steadily every time she appeared.

"She must have laid her plans then—and carried out the first part. She went to her cabin, got the ball of cord and cut off a certain length. She took it to the vacant cabin and tied it securely on the pipe— and she arranged a noose with a slipknot and laid it along the top of the pipe. Arranged that way, it would not be noticeable to anyone entering the room —or at least look like nothing more than a piece of string tied around the pipe. She placed the chair in the right position underneath and then went quietly off to bed with Lucy. She waited until Lucy was asleep and then went out and made her way to Sally's cabin.

"Sally had gone along to Peter's cabin after first undressing. She got the ring and put it on, although it was too big for her—and either Phyllis was waiting for her, when she came back, or appeared shortly afterwards. My guess is that Phyllis told her that Carla had me in her cabin and that you could see what was going on through the ventilator over the door of the connecting cabin. Sally, of course, would be all for having a look.

"I think they stood on the chair together—Sally to the fore, giggling and trying to peer through. Phyllis had only to reach up and get the prepared noose. Probably she pretended to lose her balance, clutched at Sally to steady herself and slipped the noose over Sally's head. She pushed her off the chair at the same instant—and had only to hold her arms down and watch her die.

"She was shrewd enough to realize that the cord might be traced to her—so that after Sally was dead she took the cord from Sally's bathrobe and tied it beside the other. She found, then, that she could not remove the other cord without a pair of scissors, and she had none with her. She must have known that it was dangerous not to return to her cabin immediately, but apparently she was now desperately afraid to leave the cord there.

"She thought of Carla's cabin—only one door away. She knew it was a risk to go there for scissors, but she figured that there was even greater danger in going all the way down to her own cabin and back again. She had to return there, anyway, and the fewer times she took the trip, the less likelihood there was of being seen. She knew, too, that Carla had spent the day with Peter, and since drinking figured largely in Peter's scheme of things it was highly probable that Carla had had enough to make her sleep heavily.

"She went into Carla's cabin and found a chair in front of the dressing table, where she probably knew the scissors were.

"She hadn't expected the chair, but she moved it quietly and got the scissors. She noticed Carla's dressing gown as she turned to go, and decided to put it on so that she would be mistaken for Carla in case she was seen on her way to the other cabin.

"She went back and cut the cord away—and dropped the little piece that I later found.

"Peter's ring had dropped from Sally's hand, and Phyllis picked it off the floor and dropped it into the pocket of Carla's dressing robe. Evidently she conceived the idea, at that point, of incriminating Carla, for her next move was very daring.

"She came into my cabin and deliberately woke me up. She stood just inside the door with her back to me, bending over the washbasin, and all I could see was the shimmer of satin. When I spoke she slipped out. If the fittings of the ship had been more modern she could not have done it, but she knew I had no reading light and would have to get out of bed to switch on the light.

"She went back to Carla's cabin and replaced the dressing robe and the scissors, but she forgot to return the chair to its original position.

"The next night Carla was in a state of nervous excitement after Peter's scheme for getting her to believe that the body was still in the next cabin. When she heard someone moving around in there her first thought was Sally's ghost."

I interrupted at this point to say indignantly, "I don't believe in ghosts!" but nobody paid any attention to me.

Robert went on: "It was Phyllis, trying to get in to Carla. She was badly frightened at that time. She knew that Carla had heard Sally giggle and was afraid that her own voice had been recognized. Aside from her fears, she wanted Carla out of the way because she was too much with Chet.

"The connecting door was locked, so she went around into the corridor and tried the other door but found it locked too.

"Peter had searched the empty cabin earlier in the evening—before Carla came down.

"Phyllis went back to the ladies' room that she and her sister always used. It has a ventilator which is very close to Chet's cabin—and she cried out loud.

"I figured that out last night when I had supposedly disappeared into thin air. I had noticed the ventilator right across the corridor from Chet's cabin and supposed that it led to the ladies' room near Phyllis' and Lucy's cabin. I went in to investigate—and was shortly followed by Lucy and Phyllis themselves. The investigation had not taken long, but the girls' laundry work did. Several times while I was standing on the lid of one of the toilets I regretted that I had not merely said 'Good evening' to them when they came in—and walked out.

"There is an empty box under the ventilator—I don't know what it is used for, but it was empty at that time—and Phyllis must have stood on it, so that she could cry directly through the ventilator.

"She started the crying as a bid for Chet's sympathy. I think she hoped he would ask her what was wrong, and she could tell him some tale about her parents favoring Lucy and making her own life miserable. She thought he would know where the crying was coming from and who was doing it, but her plan went astray.

"Chet thought the voice was supernatural, and Phyllis heard him say as much to Carla. The fact that he was talking to Carla at all made Phyllis more determined than ever to get rid of her.

"Before Phyllis went back to bed that night she went past her parents' room to see if the three matches she had placed in front of the door had been disturbed. She wanted to know beforehand if either of them—and particularly her mother—had left the room, so that she could tell them before they asked her some story of where she had been.

"The next night, before she murdered Kay, she placed three matches in front of my door. She thought I was doing a little too much nosing around, and she wanted to know if I had been out. It was the only time she left the matches at my door. After that she was taken up with the idea of playing ghost, rather than incriminating Carla, whom she intended to eliminate anyway. She was not so concerned with my movements then, but she was still anxious that her parents should not know she was roaming around.

"On the night Kay was murdered Phyllis did not know that she was sleeping in with Carla—but she did know that Carla had been drinking. The door was not locked, and she simply walked in. She went straight to the berth and strangled Kay with her hands—it was dark, and she naturally assumed that it was Carla. You will remember that there were some bruises on Kay's neck that were not accounted for by the cord.

"She had brought some cord with her, but this time it was a length she had snipped on in the barbershop and stolen. I heard from Lucy that Phyllis was very proud of her slipknots—and in any case she wanted to be sure of the job. She tied Kay up, as we know.

"Carla was not disturbed until Phyllis was on her way out. She had seen the dressing robe again and had put it on to get back to her own cabin. I think she intended to discard it when she got far enough away from Carla's cabin, and leave it in some public part of the ship and proceed to her own cabin. But she noticed the grey chiffon lining and remembered Chet's uneasy belief that the crying was ghostly. She decided to foster the ghost idea. She put the dressing robe on again, grey side out this time, and found that the collar was long enough to conceal her face.

"I found out from Lucy that when she and Phyllis saw the grey mist it was Phyllis who called attention to it, and Lucy admitted that she herself merely caught a glimpse of something vanishing around a corner— probably the white coat of a steward.

"When a search was started for the dressing robe Phyllis was afraid to keep it any longer, and she returned it, stuffing it into a drawer in Carla's cabin.

"I don't know what she thought when she realized that she had killed Kay instead of Carla. I don't suppose, with her nature, that she worried much about Kay, but she must have been furious at having missed up on Carla, who was eating three meals a day with Chet and talking with him more and more often.

"I got Carla to pump Mrs. Jennings, and Phyllis was curled up in a chair, listening. We found her handkerchief there—a large, practical, cheap handkerchief—she had others which were identical with it.

"Phyllis' next move was to take the dressing robe again. She had made up her mind to murder Carla, and she felt that the robe was a necessary and complete disguise. She became more careless of being seen and played up the ghost idea by crying in other ladies' rooms— always near a ventilator.

"At this time Carla's cabin was always locked at night, and Phyllis realized that she would have to go in early and hide.

"She went in just after dinner one night. She had heard Carla complain of headache and thought she might be down early on that account.

"She took the dressing robe with her, but it was too early in the evening—with too many people around—for her to wear it. I suppose she concealed it under her evening wrap, in case of emergency.

"I think she must have turned dizzy or ill after she got into Carla's cabin, for she used the smelling salts—but must have put her handkerchief around the bottle, because the only fingerprints on it were Sally's. She must have handled it at some time.

"Phyllis still felt ill, I think, and decided to go. She put on the dressing robe—inside out, with the collar over her face—and slipped out. Carla saw her.

"She recovered later and attended the dance, but she kept an eye on Carla and at last saw her go off. She did not know where she had gone, but she did know that she had said something to cause trouble between Carla and me which might keep me out of the way. She hoped Carla would drink too much and forget to lock her door.

"She came around that night after she had seen Lucy off to sleep—and brought more cord from the barbershop.

"She found the door open, but to her surprise Carla was not there. She waited for a long time and at last grew so restless that she went out.

"Carla was just coming along the corridor—and she showed fear and turned to run. Phyllis ran after her in a fury. I think her vanity was hurt by that time. It had been so easy to get Sally and Kay—and Carla had somehow eluded her consistently.

"She caught up with Carla in a dead-end corridor and frightened her into insensibility. She tied the cord around Carla's throat quickly and secured it above in a furious hurry. She was terrified at having to do it in an open corridor, and she must have heard me walking around as she finished. She probably missed me by seconds—and I got to Carla just in time.

"Now about yesterday. While Lucy was having coffee and a liqueur with Peter, Phyllis returned the robe for the last time. She had kept it locked in one of her bags, with the key around her neck. I'm convinced that she kept the diary there, too, but it isn't there now. I suppose she was afraid of the customs inspection.

"She went to have her afternoon nap with Lucy, but after Lucy was asleep she went upstairs again, to Mrs. Jennings' drawing room, and overheard Mrs. Jennings boasting of what she knew and making an appointment with Carla for four o'clock tea.

"We shall never know whether Mrs. Jennings was making a bid for the limelight or whether she really had some knowledge of what was going on. At any rate Phyllis was frightened. She had often heard Mrs. Jennings talking to Lady Marsh and knew that her store of scandal and information was astonishingly large.

"She returned to her cabin, to find Lucy just waking up, and the two of them came up to the writing room.

"Lucy could not see Phyllis unless she turned right around in her chair. She did this once, when she had addressed Phyllis and had received no answer—probably due to the fact that Phyllis was planning furiously. But Lucy told me that she had spoken to her twice, after the first time, and still had not been answered. On these occasions, however, she had not bothered to turn around but had merely clicked her tongue in annoyance and decided that Phyllis was asleep over her book.

"As a matter of fact, Phyllis wasn't there. Directly after she had seen Celia leave she had gone down to Carla's cabin to get the iron—she returned to the idea of throwing suspicion on Carla. She got a cord from a window in the corridor, a curtain tieback.

"She crept into the lounge, closing the door between that room and the writing room, and killed Mrs. Jennings by hitting her on the head several times with the iron. She tied the cord around her neck and over the back of a chair, but it was a clumsy arrangement and would have been totally ineffective. She wiped some blood from her hands— or possibly her face—with Mrs. Jennings' handkerchief and took it and the iron to Carla's cabin and stuffed them into the wardrobe. She got back to her chair in time to see Carla go in. She was extraordinarily lucky in that Carla, who had been walking the deck and looking in the windows from time to time, never once saw her."

Robert heaved a sigh. "There's not much more," he said a little wearily.

"Tonight I laid a trap for Phyllis. I had not dreamed that she would take the chance of killing Mrs. Jennings in broad daylight, in a public lounge. But she was more daring and more skillful than I had supposed.

"I kept her in sight after tea and saw her maneuver Chet off for a private talk. I followed and listened—and was in time to hear Phyllis say, 'Well, and whose address have you got?'

" 'Carla's,' said Chet briefly. 'But just think, Phyllis—it won't be long now before we can get away from all this.'

"Phyllis was silent for a moment, then she said, 'Won't you come and see us when you're in London? We'll be there for some time.'

"He agreed, and they went off.

"Later, after my session in the ladies' room, I went up and got Mr. Ogilvie to call off the search for me, and I made some arrangements with him.

"I went up on deck and found Lucy and Phyllis. They declared they were going to stay up all night and watch for the lights on shore, and I told them that that was my intention too.

"I confided to them, as a joke, that Mr. Ogilvie had locked Carla's door but had overlooked the fact that my door was open and also the connecting door between my room and Carla's.

"Phyllis excused herself shortly afterwards, and so did I.

"I figured that she would probably make another attempt on Carla—not only because Chet had her address, but also because the iron had not been found where she had stuffed it in Carla's cupboard. I suppose she thought Carla had found it first and thrown it overboard.

"I went straight down to Carla's cabin and waited—and you know the rest."

CHAPTER FORTY-SEVEN

WE SAILED THROUGH the Golden Gate that afternoon. We were all up on deck and all more or less subdued, but I think everyone felt a certain sense of relaxation.

Lady Marsh and Lucy wore black dresses, and Sir Alfred had a black tie. They stood quietly along the rail, not saying much and looking oddly pathetic. Peter had evidently made up his mind, for he stood grimly beside Lucy, his face set in lines of conventional gravity. He was smoking incessantly. As Lucy turned to him with an occasional word her manner seemed already to be faintly possessive.

Chet stood somewhat apart, still trying determinedly to throw the taste of the voyage away.

Celia was straining anxiously for the first glimpse of the dock and the friends who would be meeting her.

Mr. Imhoff, hands folded on the rail and camera hung over his shoulder, looked five years younger.

Robert and I stood together. "We have a lot of plans to make," he said idly.

"What plans?"

"For the wedding."

"Oh," I said, "are you still going to marry me?"

"Don't be an ass," he said amiably. "It was all settled the day I came on board. But it has to be broken to Aunt Edna and Uncle Henry."

"They'll say it's ridiculous."

"It is ridiculous to marry a woman who is always fainting and screaming—but I'm sorry for you. I don't know where else you could get a man."

"Robert," I said thoughtfully, "what was that sharp, tapping sound while we were waiting in the dark?"

He laughed. "Merely my impatience. I was tapping my nails against the wall."

"You nearly scared me to death," I said resentfully.

He laughed again and kissed my nose. "You'd better start thinking about your trousseau. I'm taking you back with me when I go, you know. I figure that it will be much less wearing to have you in the same cabin with me where I can keep an eye on you."

"Anything you like," I agreed, "only so you don't bring me back on this boat. I never want to see it again."

"You'll see it every time it gets in to Tahiti—there's nothing else to do there." He pressed my arm against his side. "But you needn't ride on it again."

He was silent for a while, and then he said, "What were you thinking about while you lay there waiting to be murdered?"

I blushed furiously and stared steadily down into the water. "I'll never tell you," I said firmly.

THE END

Other Rue Morgue vintage mysteries

Great Black Kanba
by Constance & Gwenyth Little

"If you love train mysteries as much as I do, hop on the Trans-Australia Railway in *Great Black Kanba*, a fast and funny 1944 novel by the talented team of Constance and Gwenyth Little. "—Jon L. Breen, *Ellery Queen's Mystery Magazine*.

"I have decided to add *Kanba* to my favorite mysteries of all time list!. . . a zany ride I'll definitely take again and again."—Diane Plumley in the Murder Ink newsletter.

A young American woman who's lost her memory comes to on board an Australian train and discovers she could be a murderer in this 1944 novel by the queens of the wacky cozy. Not only does the young woman have a bump on her head and no memory, she also has no idea how she came to be on a train crossing the Nullarbor Plain of Australia with a group of boisterous, argumentative Aussies who appear to be her relatives. Nor does she recall ever having met the young doctor who says he's her fiance. Which is a little awkward, since there's another man on the train who says she'd agreed to marry him, and a love letter in her pocketbook from yet another beau.

She also discovers that she may be a cold-blooded killer. Even worse, she may have really bad taste in clothes, given the outfit she's wearing. When some of her fellow passengers are killed, an Australian cop thinks she would make a great suspect and the only reason she isn't arrested is that the train keeps passing into other jurisdictions. The pasengers also have to keep changing trains, since each Australian state uses a different railroad gauge.

And then there's the matter of the barking lizard in her compartment. The lizard belongs to Uncle Joe, an amateur painter who awakes every morning to discover that someone has defaced his latest masterpiece. It all adds up to some delightful mischief—call it Cornell Woolrich on laughing gas—which is what you would expect from the pens of the two Australian-born Little sisters.

0-915230-22-4 $14.00

The Black Honeymoon
by Constance & Gwenyth Little

Can you murder someone with feathers? If you don't believe that feathers can kill, then you probably haven't read one of the 21 mysteries by the two Little sisters, the reigning queens of the cozy screwball mystery from the 1930s to the 1950s. No, Uncle Richard wasn't tickled to death—though we can't make the same guarantee for readers—but the hyper-allergic rich man did manage to sneeze himself into the hereafter in his hospital room.

Suspicion falls on his nurse, young Miriel Mason, who recently married the dead man's nephew, Ian Ross, an army officer on furlough. Ian managed to sweep Miriel off her feet and to the altar—well, at least to city hall—before she had a chance to check his bank balance, which was nothing to boast about. In fact, Ian cheerfully explains that they'll have to honeymoon in the old family mansion and hope that his relations can leave the two lovebirds alone.

But when Miriel discovers that Ian's motive for marriage may have had nothing to do with her own charms, she decides to postpone at least one aspect of the honeymoon, installing herself and her groom in separate bedrooms. To clear herself of Richard's murder, Miriel summons private detective Kelly, an old crony of her father's, who gets himself hired as a servant in the house even though he can't cook, clean or serve. While Kelly snoops, the body count continues to mount at an alarming rate. Nor is Miriel's hapless father much help. Having squandered the family fortune, he now rents out rooms in his mansion and picks up a little extra cash doing Miriel's laundry.

Originally published in 1944, *The Black Honeymoon* is filled with tantalizing questions: Who is moaning in the attic? What is the terrible secret in the family Bible? Why does Aunt Violet insist on staying in her room? Will Kelly get fired for incompetence before he nabs the killer? Will Miriel and Ian ever consummate their marriage? Combining the charm and laughs of a Frank Capra movie with the eccentric characters of a George S. Kaufmann play, *The Black Honeymoon* is a delight from start to finish.   **0-915230-21-6 $14.00**

The Black Gloves
by Constance & Gwenyth Little

"I'm relishing every madcap moment."—*Murder Most Cozy*

Welcome to the Vickers estate near East Orange, New Jersey, where the middle class is destroying the neighborhood, erecting their horrid little cottages, playing on the Vickers tennis court, and generally disrupting the comfortable life of Hammond Vickers no end.

It's bad enough that he had to shell out good money to get his daughter Lissa a divorce in Reno only to have her brute of an ex-husband show up on his doorstep. But why does there also have to be a corpse in the cellar? And lights going on and off in the attic?

Lissa, on the other hand, welcomes the newcomers into the neighborhood, having spotted a likely candidate for a summer beau among them. But when she hears coal being shoveled in the cellar and finds a blue dandelion near a corpse, what's a girl gonna do but turn detective, popping into people's cottages and dipping dandelions into their inkwells looking for a color match. And she'd better catch the killer fast, because Detective Sergeant Timothy Frobisher says that only a few nail files are standing between her and jail.

Originally published in 1939, *The Black Gloves* was one of 21 wacky mysteries written by the Little sisters and is a sparkling example of the light-hearted cozy mystery that flourished between the Depression and the Korean War. It won't take you long to understand why these long out-of-print titles have so many ardent fans.   **0-915230-20-8 $14.00**

The Rue Morgue Press intends to eventually publish all 21 of the Little mysteries.

Death at The Dog
by Joanna Cannan
In the tradition of
Sayers, Christie, Tey, Allingham and Marsh

**Murder in an English village pub during a
World War II blackout**
**"An excellent English rural tale." —Jacques Barzun &
Wendell Hertig Taylor in *A Catalogue of Crime***

Set in late 1939 during the first anxious months of World War II, Joanna Cannan's *Death at The Dog*, originally published in 1941, is a wonderful example of the classic English detective novel that first flourished between the two World Wars when writers like Agatha Christie, Dorothy L. Sayers and Ngaio Marsh began practicing their trade. Like so many books of its period, *Death at The Dog* is set in a picturesque village filled with thatched-roof cottages, eccentric villagers and genial pubs. As well-plotted as a Christie, with clues abundantly and fairly planted, it's also as deftly written as the best of the books by either Sayers or Marsh, filled with quotable lines and perceptive observations on the human condition. Cannan had a gift for characterization that's second to none in Golden Age detective fiction, and she created two memorable lead characters in *Death at The Dog*.

One of them is Inspector Guy Northeast, a lonely young Scotland Yard inspector who makes his second and final appearance here and finds himself hopelessly smitten with the chief suspect in the murder of the village tyrant. The other unforgettable character is the "lady novelist" Crescy Hardwick, an unconventional and ultimately unobtainable woman a number of years Guy's senior, who is able to pierce his armor and see the unhappiness that haunts the detective's private moments. Well aware that all the evidence seems to point to her, she is also able—unlike her less imaginative fellow villagers—to see how very good Northeast is at his job.

0-915230-23-2 $14.00

Murder, Chop Chop
by James Norman

"The book has the butter-wouldn't-melt-in-his-mouth cool of Rick in *Casablanca*." —*The Rocky Mountain News*. "Amuses the reader no end."—*Mystery News*. "This long out-of-print masterpiece is intricately plotted, full of eccentric characters and very humorous indeed. Highly recommended."—*Mysteries by Mail*

You'll find a cipher or two to crack, a train with a mind of its own, and Chiang Kai-shek's false teeth to cloud the waters in this 1942 classic tale of detection and adventure set during the Sino-Japanese war, with the sleuthing honors going to a gigantic Mexican guerrilla fighter named Gimiendo Quinto and a beautiful Eurasian known as Mountain of Virtue.

0-915230-16-X $13.00

Cook Up a Crime
by Charlotte Murray Russell

"Some wonderful old-time recipes...highly recommended."—*Mysteries by Mail.*

Meet Jane Amanda Edwards, a self-styled "full-fashioned" spinster who complains she hasn't looked at herself in a full-length mirror since Helen Hokinson started drawing for *The New Yorker.* But you can always count on Jane to look into other people's affairs, especially when there's a juicy murder case to investigate. In this 1951 title Jane goes looking for recipes (included between chapters) and finds a body instead. As usual, in one of the longest running jokes in detective fiction, her lily-of-the-field brother Arthur is found clutching the murder weapon.

0-915230-18-6 $13.00

The Man from Tibet
by Clyde B. Clason

"The novels of American classicist Clason have been unavailable for years, a lapse happily remedied with the handsome trade paperback reprint of (Westborough's) best known case. Clason spun ornate puzzles in the manner of Carr and Queen and spread erudition as determinedly as Van Dine."—Jon L. Breen, *Ellery Queen's Mystery Magazine.* "A highly original and practical locked-room murder method."— Robert C.S. Adey.

The elderly historian, Professor Theocritus Lucius Westborough, solves a cozy 1938 locked room mystery involving a Tibetan lama in Chicago in which the murder weapon may well be an eighth century manuscript. The result is a fair-play puzzler for fans of John Dickson Carr. With an extensive bibliography, it is also one of the first popular novels to examine in depth then-forbidden Tibet and Tibetan Buddhism.

0-915230-17-8 $14.00

Murder is a Collector's Item
by Elizabeth Dean

"Completely enjoyable."—*New York Times.* "Fast and funny."—*The New Yorker. "Murder is a Collector's Item* froths over with the same effervescent humor as the best Hepburn-Grant films."— Sujata Massey, Agatha-award-winning author of *The Salaryman's Wife* and *Zen Attitude.*

Twenty-six-year-old Emma Marsh isn't much at spelling or geography and perhaps she butchers the odd literary quotation or two, but she's a keen judge of character and more than able to hold her own when it comes to selling antiques or solving murders. When she stumbles upon the body of a rich collector on the floor of the Boston antiques shop where she works, suspicion quickly falls upon her missing boss. Emma knows Jeff Graham is no murderer, but veteran homicide cop Jerry Donovan doesn't share her conviction.

With a little help from Hank Fairbanks, her wealthy boyfriend and would-be criminologist, Emma turns sleuth and cracks the case, but not before a host of cops, reporters and customers drift through the shop on Charles Street, trading insults and sipping scotch as they talk clues, prompting a *New York Times* reviewer to remark that Emma "drinks far more than a nice girl should."

Emma does a lot of things that women didn't do in detective novels of the 1930s. In an age of menopausal spinsters, deadly sirens, admiring wives and air-headed girlfriends, pretty, big-footed Emma Marsh stands out. She's a precursor of the independent women sleuths that finally came into their own in the last two decades of this century.

Originally published in 1939, *Murder is a Collector's Item* was the first of three books featuring Emma. Smoothly written and sparkling with dry, sophisticated humor, it combines an intriguing puzzle with an entertaining portrait of a self-possessed young woman on her own in Boston toward the end of the Great Depression. Author Dean, who worked in a Boston antiques shop, offers up an insider's view of what that easily impressed *Times* reviewer called the "goofy" world of antiques. Lovejoy, the rogue antiques dealer in Jonathan Gash's mysteries, would have loved Emma.

0-915230-19-4 $14.00

Our only non-vintage book has long been a readers' favorite

The Mirror
by Marlys Millhiser

"Completely enjoyable."—*Library Journal*. "A great deal of fun."—*Publishers Weekly*.

How could you not be intrigued, as one reviewer pointed out, by a novel in which "you find the main character marrying her own grandfather and giving birth to her own mother?" Such is the situation in Marlys Millhiser's classic novel (a Mystery Guild selection originally published by Putnam in 1978) of two women who end up living each other's lives after they look into an antique Chinese mirror.

Twenty-year-old Shay Garrett is not aware that she's pregnant and is having second thoughts about marrying Marek Weir when she's suddenly transported back 78 years in time into the body of Brandy McCabe, her own grandmother, who is unwillingly about to be married off to miner Corbin Strock. Shay's in shock but she still recognizes that the picture of her grandfather that hangs in the family home doesn't resemble her husband-to-be. But marry Corbin she does and off she goes to the high mining town of Nederland, where this thoroughly modern young woman has to learn to cope with such things as wood cooking stoves and—to her—old-fashioned attitudes about sex. Shay's ability to see into the future has her mother-in-law thinking she's a witch and others calling her a psychic but Shay was an indifferent student at best and not all of her predictions hit the mark: remember that "day of infamy" when the Japanese attacked Pearl Harbor—Dec. *11*, 1941?

In the meantime, Brandy McCabe is finding it even harder to cope with life in the Boulder, Colorado, of 1978. After all, her wedding is about to be postponed due to her own death—at least the death of her former body—at the age of 98. And, in spite of the fact she's a virgin, she's about to give birth. And *this* young woman does have some very old-fashioned ideas about sex, which leaves her husband-to-be—and father of her child—very puzzled. *The Mirror* is even more of a treat for today's readers, given that it is now a double trip back in time. Not only can readers look back on life at the turn of the century, they can also revisit the days of disco and the sexual revolution of the 1970's.

So how does one categorize *The Mirror*? Is it science fiction? Fantasy? Supernatural? Mystery? Romance? Historical fiction? You'll find elements of each but in the end it's a book driven by that most magical of all literary devices: imagine if...

.   0-915230-15-1 $14.95

About The Rue Morgue Press

The Rue Morgue Press Classic Mystery line is designed to bring back into print those books that were favorites of readers between the turn of the century and 1960. The editors welcome suggestions for reprints. To receive our catalog or to make suggestions, write The Rue Morgue Press, P.O. Box 4119, Boulder, Colorado 80306.